BEN JACKSON

THE
BEFORE

Published by Indie Publishing Group

ISBN: 978-0-9952340-7-9

Interior and Cover by Indie Publishing Group

To my wife. Without you, my life wouldn't be the amazing roller coaster ride that it is.

For all your hard work and commitment, love you always!

PROLOGUE

The deer walked through the forest, his large, powerful body imposing on the smaller things around him. Over the last few years, life had been much better for him and his family. The hunters hadn't bothered them much at all, the large noisy machines even less. That didn't mean that he had time to relax; the herd still needed his guidance, support, and knowledge.

His senses started to fire into his brain, rapidly shooting adrenaline to all points of his body, telling him something wasn't right in the forest around him. He wasn't sure exactly what was wrong, but finely-tuned instincts took over.

Run! his mind screamed, *run now!*

CHAPTER 1

Damn it. Two hours wasted tracking the deer only to lose it over the hard ground; Dylan was angry at himself. It seemed the animals adapted to change a lot quicker than people. Dylan was a mature twenty year old, big for his age, broad shoulders, well-defined chest and large, strong arms.

You had to be in these terrible times; the weak didn't last long. It had been ten years since everything changed, the Before, that's what the younger kids were calling it, those too young to remember how easy life had been. One word, Before; it hardly did justice to what had happened and where they all found themselves now. His parents were gone; he looked after his younger brother, Seb, and his sister, Brea. They lived in a compound with a small group of survivors, all decent folk who looked after each other as much as possible. With a sigh Dylan started heading back to the compound; at least the walk would give him some time to think. Ha, Dylan laughed to himself, that's one thing there was plenty of these days, time. The only problem with time was you couldn't eat it, you couldn't turn it back, and it wouldn't stop you from dying.

No one really knows what exactly led up to that day back in 2027. Sure, plenty of people have speculated over the years, and we know some of the facts, but there was just so much that had happened in such a short time. Whatever it was, we probably won't ever know for sure. What we all do know are the eventual results: death, famine, disease, and a breakdown in civilization on such a widespread scale that we, the human race, may never recover. A small amount of people living in a world that was only a shadow of what it once was. Technology had led to the earth being at its highest ever point of overpopulation; some even said what happened was perhaps evolution's way of saving the few by getting rid of the many. Whatever it was, it meant that the rest of us would suffer for the mistakes of those that came before us. We are the ones who will have to live with it, or die with it.

What started as an outbreak of the Cinam virus in a poverty stricken area of Africa quickly spread to every continent on the planet. Leave it to nature to leave a chink in the armor, a small weakness that a tiny virus could crawl through, leaving a trail of death and decay in its path. This in itself wasn't a major problem, most countries above the poverty line had strategies and dynamic plans in place to deal with the Cinam virus, what they weren't prepared for was the mutation from Cinam to Cinam2x. Carefully prepared plans went out the window once the virus became airborne, added to that its mortality rate moved into the high ninety percent of all those who found themselves infected by it, and there were a lot of those.

Passive containment was initially tried, a great idea that

many countries placed their hope in, but failed; the incubation period was seven days before any symptoms presented. It was just too long between someone becoming infected and authorities being able to identify that they were sick. Flu-like coughs, deep racking fits, fever, and, eventually, massive organ failure rapidly occurred within twenty-four hours.

A more aggressive approach was undertaken. Isolation of entire towns and cities, the transportation hub was shut down, planes were grounded and all movement severely restricted upon the threat of death. The military was called in; National Guard units were mobilized, and complete martial law was declared. Anyone caught trying to break out of containment was killed. There were no questions, no detainment, and no arrest; if they found you, they killed you.

Infrastructure started to fail. Gas and oil stopped flowing from the Middle East, and the small local reserves were quickly exhausted. The government's much talked about reserves were grossly inadequate. Without fuel, and the specialists to maintain energy production, mass nationwide power outages quickly followed. Water, sewerage, power, telecommunications, and transportation all collapsed under overloaded pressure from lack of maintenance and the knowledgeable people to maintain them.

Communities started to break down. People moved further away from the big cities and tried to establish themselves in smaller safe enclaves where they had just a slightly better chance of survival. Those people who survived the initial ravages of Cinam2x became known as the ten percenters; they didn't know if they were lucky to be spared a quick death or unlucky to have been sentenced to a slower slide into despair, hunger, rape, and eventual death. The ones who survived had a natural immunity to the virus, which was probably passed down through the generations over the last thousand years. It was strange how nature could engineer a virus killing machine, but with a small twist, just one strand of DNA meant the difference between life and death. Things many people had forgotten long ago due to laziness or the advance of technology now became essential to survival: hunting, foraging, harvesting, tracking, and scavenging were all now needed if you wanted even the slightest chance to survive in this hostile environment.

A lot had changed, but in some ways, nothing had changed. Dylan reflected as he closed in on his home. Given half a chance, many of the people would cut someone's throat for something to eat. There were new rules now, none. You lived however you lived, or you died, quickly or painfully. It didn't matter; the result was the same, blackness, nothing.

Dylan whistled twice as he approached the tall, rusting gates of the compound, and then paused. Things had been quiet recently, but it paid to be safe, and they had certain safeguards set in place for a reason. He wouldn't forgive the person who endangered the life of his friends or family, and would expect none in return. Not everyone these days lived by honest means. There were plenty of armed groups who lived by taking what others struggled to live off. The powerful still attempted to prey on the weak, even at a much smaller scale; would people never learn? Maybe it was the animal inside us; it just happened to be more prevalent in some people.

A few months before, they had been forced to defend themselves against a group of armed strangers who thought they looked like an easy target. Dylan looked up at what remained of three of the strangers, which were still hanging from trees along the perimeter. This small notice had been voted on by the community, a grizzly reminder to those who thought that it would be easier to take instead of earn. Dylan heard the double reply whistle from above the walls, slowly stood up from where he was crouched in the trees and headed in towards the gate, bow in hand, but otherwise empty-handed. He wouldn't be eating fresh venison steaks tonight, but he wouldn't go hungry either. His sister, Brea, would have made a stew from the dried meat they had stored, as well as some of the vegetables which they had managed to grow in the communal gardens.

"No luck, Dylan?" Frank yelled loudly from the top of the wall, his deep voice seeming damn loud compared to the quiet of the forest Dylan had just left.

Dylan shook his head slowly from side to side, rubbing his jaw, and yelled in reply, "Not today Frank, but there's always tomorrow. You know what they say; time is one thing we are all rich in!" Frank just laughed and went back to watching his part of the forest. After a while, it all blurred into one big patch of green, but like Dylan had said, "What else was there to do?"

As Dylan walked through the compound, he smiled and nodded to the people who were out and about. No one begrudged the lack of fresh meat; Dylan always provided more than his fair share. As he entered his shared house, he unstrung the bow; it weakened the string of the bow to leave it strung all the time, and placed it along with his arrows next to the door. It didn't matter where he had been or how much of a hurry he was in; he always placed it in the same place. This way it was easy to reach, and he knew exactly where it would be when or if he needed it. Routine played a strong part in survival; if you knew where something would be, in an emergency, it would be much easier to find.

"No luck then, big brother?" Brea asked from the kitchen with a positive sound to her voice. No matter how desperate things were, she would never make her brother feel he had failed or let them down.

"No, little sister, just like you said, the heat kept them deep in the forest, they were all just too skittish today," Dylan said as he pulled one of the stools up and heavily sat down. It wasn't until he sat down and relaxed inside his home that he realized just how tense he was outside the walls of the compound. Once again his sister had been right, and, as usual, it irritated him just a little bit. He prided himself on his hunting and ability to provide for not only his small family but also the families inside the compound walls. He knew there was probably no one who could have done better; his accuracy with the bow, and hunting and tracking skills were second to none in the compound.

"You'll do better tomorrow, the stores aren't that low, and winter is still a little way off yet. We still have some time left to stock up on meat. Have you had any luck scrounging?" Dylan was one of the compound's best scroungers or scavengers. He wasn't particularly great at it, but it was probably due more to the fact that he traveled the furthest away from the compound while hunting, and maybe just a little bit of good old-fashioned luck.

"No, not today. I'm going to head west tomorrow towards the old highway and have a look around to see if there's something, anything really, that's been missed," Dylan replied.

His legs were starting to ache since he had sat down to eat his dinner. It had been a long day with an even longer one in store for him tomorrow. After he had finished dinner with his brother and sister, he said goodnight and headed towards his bed. Shrugging his top off, but leaving everything else on, he threw himself onto his bed, within minutes of lying down he drifted off to sleep, his head full of thoughts of a time before when things were easier, and life held so much promise.

Dylan didn't really remember the weeks leading up to his parents' death. Everyone was panicking. Schools had closed. The military was openly patrolling the streets day and night, collecting bodies from outside houses and burning them and the houses they came from. His mother and father both got sick so quickly, both hoping against all hope it was just a cold or flu, but deep down inside they both knew better, and so did Dylan. Dylan's Uncle Stephen showed up to take him, his brother, and sister. His uncle had already lost his family and survived; the lucky one perhaps, or not, whatever way you decided to look at it. He would have given his own life just to save any one of his children. He knew a place where survivalists were setting up and he could get them in. That had been almost ten years ago; dates weren't so important these days. His uncle had been killed a few years ago while hunting, but he had managed to pass on everything he had known to his nephews and niece before he was killed. A Wilder had killed him. Wilders was the name they gave to the solo, almost savage wanderers. They had found his body after he hadn't returned on time. From what they managed to work out from the tracks, it was just one man. Dylan lost the track three days later; the rain set in and the trail he followed went cold. He cast around a further day hoping to pick up any sign of the killer, but without luck. His uncle was buried up behind the hills looking down on the compound, nothing but a rough cross to mark where he lay. With these somber thoughts filling his head, Dylan drifted off to a troubled sleep. In this day and age, rarely was a night's sleep not troubled.

CHAPTER 2

He set off early before sunrise. He had a long day ahead, and it wouldn't pay to spend the first part of it lying in his bed wasting good traveling time.

"Dylan! Dylan, you want a hand today with hunting?" The shout startled him out of his thoughts, this close to the compound he wasn't paying as much attention as he should have. *That's what got you killed.* The shout had come from Matt, who was probably the closest thing Dylan had to a best friend.

"Hey, Matt, sure. I'm heading out west to the highway today if you're interested," Dylan replied.

"Sure man, you know me, I'm easy. Besides, I have some of those new arrows I'm interested in testing. You see much animal activity on your hunts over the last few days?" Matt asked.

"No, not a lot happening close to the compound at all lately, but that will probably change once this weather changes. I'm hoping it will be quiet all the way out and back today, but we may have to rack up somewhere near the highway depending on how things turn out," Dylan replied. Never one to go out of his way to look for trouble, Dylan hoped this would be another easy run in and out, but you never knew when you headed out towards the highway. It was one of the worst places for him to go and he would normally avoid it if he could. The abandoned cars, trucks, and campers out on the highway were a gold mine of supplies and essential items. Before, everyone had taken them for granted, but not anymore. The problem with the highway was it tended to draw more than just the odd scrounger or survivor. Wilders and other armed groups followed the highways looking for easy pickings, and they didn't mess around.

"Okay, Matt, let's head out. I'll take the point. You drop back a little way until we clear the first set of woods and then we'll close up." Dylan's natural ability to lead, and his position in the compound as one of the best hunters, meant people were normally happy to let him take charge once they were over the walls. They both adjusted their packs and set out in a westerly direction. They would throw a wide loop to make sure anyone who picked them up wouldn't be able to easily track them back to the compound. Dylan was hoping to cut the highway sometime around midday, all going well, and then follow that as long as possible depending on whatever they discovered there. Matt had walked into the compound almost five years ago, as far as Dylan could remember. His easy-going nature and friendly attitude had guaranteed him a place almost from the first day he had walked in. He didn't lack in skills either, having survived alone for almost a year. Matt was an excellent shot with his compound bow and his wood skills were fantastic; they had to have been for him not to have been picked up. That wasn't what he contributed most to the compound, though; Matt was great with his hands. He had that natural instinct on how things ran and worked, and better yet, how to pull them apart and fix them. Matt had fit in well with Dylan and his family, and, more often than not, could be found sharing an evening meal with them or helping Brea around the house they all shared. He was quick with a joke or a smile, but behind that cheeky lopsided grin, he had shared the same pain which all of them had.

Brea hadn't heard Dylan leave the house this morning. She was usually a very light sleeper, any little noise would normally have had her awake, but the fact Dylan hadn't woken her wasn't that unusual. That guy walked through most places like a ghost, you almost swore you could see something or hear something, but if he didn't want to be seen or heard, he wouldn't be.

"Seb! Your breakfast is ready. Wash up and come down and have something to eat," Brea shouted from the kitchen. She had already been up and about for almost two hours, drawn their water ration from the tanks, and collected the eggs from the chickens down by the pens. She wished Dylan would have stayed for breakfast, but she might as well be wishing for the sky to be purple for all the good that would do.

"Seb, breakfast now!" she yelled, irritation beginning to creep into her voice. Every morning they played the same stupid game, and it wasn't helping her mood at all this morning. Brea always worried when Dylan went out, and more so when she knew that he was going towards the highway. That was where their uncle had been killed, and there was no way she wanted to have to bury someone else whom she loved. As if that wasn't enough, to top it off she was pretty sure Matt would have gone with him. You would think that with the two of them it would ease her troubles, but trouble just seemed to find those two no matter how hard they tried to avoid it.

"Okay, okay, I'm up, Brea." Seb chuckled as he walked into the small kitchen and pulled up a stool, sighing as he sat down.

"I'm getting pretty damn sick of this, Seb! You think I don't have anything better to do than spend my time waiting on you and dragging your sorry butt out of bed!? Your brother and Matt are both up and gone, most likely they won't return tonight, either, so I'm going to need a hand, okay?" Brea raised her eyebrow and threw an icy stare at her younger brother, just daring him to try to dodge out of helping her today.

"Sure, sis, umm, that is absolutely no problem," Seb replied, as if he would dare try anything else. He did have plans today, too; he had been building his own bow and wanted to surprise his brother and Matt with it when they returned. He knew how hard they both worked and wanted to be able to help out around the place a bit more. He just hated helping his sister.

It wasn't Seb's fault, he was just a typical teen, and just because the world had gone to crap it didn't change his attitude that much. Brea was hoping he would soon outgrow it and step up to assume more responsibility around the compound, following in his elder brother's and Matt's footsteps. Seb hadn't grown up in the Before; he was only three when disaster had changed everyone's destinies. Brea didn't know if he was lucky he couldn't miss something he didn't know, or unlucky he never got to experience it like all the rest of them had. There wasn't a lot to talk about as they both sat down to eat their omelets. They ate in silence as they thought, both thinking about the two people dearest to them, outside the walls. Matt and Dylan out in the wild together, facing whatever came their way. Brea and Seb were no strangers to death and loss, but neither could bear thinking of what it would be like without Matt and Dylan. Although neither of them was that religious, it wouldn't hurt to whisper a few quick prayers.

Dylan and Matt crouched in the tree line, about a stone's throw away from the highway, scanning the abandoned cars, watching and listening. They had both been sitting there almost half an hour now; only fools rushed in, a lesson they all had to learn the hard way these days.

"You ready to move, Matt? It seems pretty quiet; we might as well make a start." Dylan wished they had more daylight left. He hadn't been out to this part of the highway before, and it had taken the two of them longer than he had expected to make it this far.

"You take the right side of the highway, Matt; I'll take this side, remember to keep an eye on your side of the woods and whistle if you need me, okay?" Matt just nodded and headed off. Dylan wasn't too worried; he knew in a pinch Matt could handle himself, and, with his compound bow, he was deadly. Dylan headed straight towards a large RV, someone's home in better times. It had the doors hanging off, and the front windscreen was smashed in. It was pretty clear to Dylan that someone had already been through, maybe several different groups over the years, but that didn't mean it wouldn't contain that one useful item. The interior of the RV was dusty; there were no footprints in the dust, and no one had been through it for quite some time. Dylan was still careful to leave it as undisturbed as possible; it paid to be careful. There was no reason to leave signs everywhere that shouted that anyone had been here. As he started opening and closing drawers and cupboards, Dylan was hoping the rest of the highway wasn't as picked clean as this RV. He found some old knives, forks, and spoons at the back of a dusty cupboard; they weren't very valuable, but any metal utensils could always be useful at the compound. He wrapped them with a piece of rag and a rubber band to stop them rattling and making noise in his pack while he was on the move. He slowly and carefully stepped out of the RV and moved along to a rusting red sedan. As he walked, he threw a quick look around the tree line checking for any unwanted guests. He pulled a small screwdriver out of his pack; he used it to pop the trunk lock on the sedan and have a look inside. Hmm, not a lot. Whoever was driving this car trying to get out of town hadn't had much time to pack, but he wasn't surprised. So many people back then had just stuffed whatever they could get into their car or nothing, and then got the hell out of town as quickly as possible. Dylan lifted the trunk liner. Bingo, he thought to himself. He looked at the car jack, tire iron, wrench, screwdrivers, and some other assorted tools. Tools were extremely useful, with no manufacturing industry to speak of and no way to just grab tools from the local hardware store, anything they needed either had to be made from scratch or scavenged.

POP, POP, POP–the loud sound of three gunshots shattered the quiet of the forest.

Dylan and Matt instantly hit the ground, arrows knocked, scanning the tree line carefully from side to side, one section at a time. No birds whistling, nothing. The whole section of the highway had gone unnaturally quiet.

"How far away do you put those shots, Matt?" Dylan whispered under his breath, as quietly as possible.

"One-mile maximum, sometimes hard to place with gunshots. The trees around us are so damn thick; they are acting as natural sound barriers. Whoever it was, they weren't aiming at us, but either way, someone or something is having a bad day." Matt frowned. There goes the quick sneak onto the highway; now they had some idiot blasting away in the forest. Gunshots were considered a last resort, they may save your life initially, but the attention could end up killing you if the wrong person or people heard them. They both stayed crouched low and moved slowly back off the highway, dodging in among the cars, no sound, no sudden unnecessary moves, and keeping as low as possible. They didn't want to stand up straight; they used the silhouettes of the cars and vans to hide them as much as possible. Once they were back in cover off the highway they had a minute to slow their breathing, let the adrenaline stop pumping, and make the decisions they needed to make.

Matt looked at Dylan; he had that damn *curiosity killed the cat* expression on his face. He could already hear the words before Dylan even started speaking.

"You want to check that out, Matt? I put it slightly to the west of us and not too far off. There are still a couple of hours of daylight and we aren't going to make it back to the compound tonight anyway." Dylan looked over Matt's shoulder as he spoke, his eyes constantly scanning all around them, never staying focused on one particular part of the forest.

Dylan used an old hunting trick while he scanned. If anything took his interest, he tried not to stare directly at it, instead allowing his peripheral vision to highlight any movement. The gunfire alone was rare these days, rare enough to warrant a look and see. Soon after the panic had set in, gunshots would be heard all the time; after the first couple of years, ammunition became much rarer, and people went back to the old-fashioned weapons from many centuries ago. Bows were easier to maintain, and you could produce your own arrows if you had the skill. They were also silent; no one would have heard Matt or him if they had been forced to shoot their bows.

"Okay, man, but slow and steady. If it doesn't smell right, we'll get the hell out of Dodge pronto. Do you want to take point? I'll watch our back trail. You find anything useful? I got some canned meat and pasta, only nine years out of date and also a pretty good little utility knife. You know the one? It has a screwdriver and crap on it. Oh yeah, I got two of those metal camping drinking bottles." Matt smiled. The knife he would keep for himself. His own was well-worn and had been sharpened so many times the blade was almost paper thin.

"No, not a lot, some cutlery and tools. Someone had picked most of this stretch of highway pretty clean, not recently, but still not much good for us. If we have time, we can come back and take another look. Anyway, let's head out, stay in sight, and signal if you see anything," Dylan said with a look of concentration etched into his rugged features.

His adrenaline was pumping now, all of his senses firing quickly, ready for whatever came their way. They both moved off into the woods, eyes scanning all around them, never focusing on one particular spot for too long. Over the years both of them had been forced to kill in self-defense, or to defend someone they knew. Neither liked it, and didn't speak about it a lot, but you had to do what needed to be done, and some people just couldn't be reasoned with. Over the last twelve months, a very rough form of order was trying to be established across the country. They hadn't made it this far out into the countryside yet, but word still spread, from Wanderers and travelers. Everyone was hoping that one day they could raise children and families without the feeling that death or starvation waited just around the corner for them. From what they had all heard, there were at least four different factions in separate parts of the country, all claiming to be the new government, and all expected to be the only government. Dylan and Matt covered the distance quickly. They didn't mess around in the woods and approached a small hill with a creek winding around its base. Dylan put his hand up, fist closed; both stopped and dropped down into a crouch. Matt made his way up to where Dylan was crouched and looked in the direction Dylan was looking; trying to work out what had grabbed Dylan's attention.

"Well, damn, that explains the gunshots; he really was desperate!" Matt shook his head as he spoke, reaching for his canteen for a quick mouthful of water. A giant brown bear was lying down next to a man licking at its neck, and trying to stand, but every time it tried, its back legs collapsed underneath it, and it groaned in pain.

"That guy must have only wounded it and then tried to run. Let's put that bear out of its misery. It's too bloody big and heavy for us to take all of it, but we will take what we can and see what he has of any use. He won't need any of it anymore, anyway," Dylan said with a shake of his head.

That guy must have been starving to try and kill a bear, or the bear had been starving. He would never have tried to kill a bear alone, not even with Matt. Bears were just too big to carry away and the meat would spoil or attract other predators before they could return for another load. Not to mention the fact that bears were notoriously hard to kill alone.

"Can you put it down?" Dylan asked. "I'll back you up if your first shot misses."

Matt just looked at him and nodded. They both moved down towards the bear, not too quickly—they didn't want it to know they were there, no matter how wounded it looked, but not wasting time either; they weren't the only predators out in the world. Those gunshots would have been heard for miles around. Dylan wanted to get what they could and get the hell away from here.

CHAPTER 3

As Brea was walking slowly through the compound, her head was miles away, probably 100 or so, if she had to guess. She couldn't help but worry when her brother, Dylan, was out hunting, especially when he had taken Matt. As if that wasn't enough, to top it all off, it looked like they wouldn't be making it back home to the compound tonight. They didn't often stay out overnight, so she shouldn't worry, she kept telling herself, but it was still very hard not to. Over the last ten years, she had seen so many people she loved and cared for hurting or killed. Brea was heading towards the compound's council rooms, damn that brother of hers! As Dylan was away hunting with Matt, it fell on her to take his place; no matter how hard she tried she just couldn't get Dylan to attend! He was always busy! If he wasn't hunting, then Matt and he were always coming up with one reason or another to avoid the meetings, no matter how flimsy they were. Grr, she shook her head, a frown creasing her normally pretty face. Dylan had turned dodging council meetings into an art form. To him, they were just too much talking; he couldn't stand all the debates and arguments. The council was made up of ten members of the compound and they normally rotated, depending on who was in the compound at the time. They tried to meet at least once a week, but more often than not, it was once a fortnight, and even then Dylan managed to be conveniently away hunting, fishing, searching, or anything else he could come up with. Lately, her thoughts had been drifting away to better times, fancy weddings, parties, and dances! She liked to imagine she and Matt getting married one day, a couple of kids, a small house, and maybe even a dog running around, but first she had to build up the courage to even tell Matt how she felt.

"Brea! Brea, hello, no Dylan again I see?" Anthony asked, with his usual abrupt and condescending manner. Brea shook her head, "No, Anthony, he's away with Matt, they were heading out to check the old west highway. They haven't been out there for a while and wanted to try and get one more run in for any useful supplies before the weather gets too cold." As if he didn't know what Dylan was up to, but, as usual, he had to try and rub it in that Dylan was missing another meeting.

"Well, no bother, but I think I speak for the entire council when I say we would all like to see him once this year! Try and mention it to him when he returns, please. Not that you aren't very welcome, and much prettier! But, we do value his opinion, and there is the matter of the fences to discuss." Anthony hardly waited for an answer before turning and walking into the meeting room.

Really? Brea thought, he was quite rude, and prettier!? The nerve of him, if he had his way, all the women would be doing was washing, cooking, and cleaning! As Brea walked in and sat down she couldn't believe this could just go on forever, something had to change. Not that things were horrible in the compound, but she always dreamed of something better. The council was discussing routine matters today, clearing the forest away from the fences to improve visibility, and just a general inspection of them to make sure they were secure. Brea just sat and grimaced, nodded along; she had other things more important than this to be worrying about. As they all agreed and no one had anything else to talk about, they agreed to meet again next week. Brea hardly let them finish speaking before she rushed out! Free from the council, Brea headed for her rooms and back to her daydreaming about Matt and worrying about Dylan.

CHAPTER 4

Dylan had heard the dull thud of the arrow before he noticed Matt had even taken his shot; it followed just as quickly with another, almost touching the first. He raised his eyebrows at Matt, questioningly.

"Better to be safe than sorry, eh?" Matt replied with a chuckle and a cheeky grin. Dylan was once again reminded of how impressed he was with Matt's shooting; two shots almost touching, and the bear was probably dead before the second arrow found its mark.

"Okay, let's get down there and see what we can find, just keep an eye out and keep listening. I don't want another bear or something worse catching us out here in the open." Dylan was already planning which way to go if anything did happen; no doubt Matt would be, too. They both headed down to the bear. Dylan checked the stranger's pulse, just to make sure, but he really was a mess and checking his pulse was more of a precaution than a necessity at this point. Matt ran his knife in along his arrow shaft and then proceeded to cut them both free from the bear. They were valuable and time-consuming to make, so if they could, they always retrieved them. Rolling the bear carcass over together, they started to work, skinning and cleaning the carcass, working as quickly as possible. This far from camp meant they wouldn't be able to take much of the meat without it spoiling, but the fur would last until they got back and could cure it. Almost an hour later, with the bear skinned and both having washed in the stream, Dylan went over to the stranger and started to go through his backpack and clothes. It was a strange feeling going through another man's entire belongings, everything he owned in his life packed into a bag, never being able to take more than he could carry. The rifle was in decent condition and would be valuable for as long as they could get the ammunition for it. He worked the magazine free, checked to make sure it was unloaded, and then put it to one side; twenty rounds left in another spare magazine also went on the ground next to it. Two knives, bowls, cutlery, and rolls of electrical wire and a few odd bolts were in a pouch, which he also laid aside. What he found next was interesting; a broken-down pistol in a leather pouch, also with four spare magazines and probably a dozen rounds of 9mm ammunition, all oiled and well cared for. Several different sets of clothes, jackets, pants, socks, and a decent set of gloves he put with the weapons, and a raincoat he threw aside. It was almost ruined and not worth carrying. Dylan started to repack it all back into the backpack; he was keeping that, and then he moved over to the stranger. This part he didn't like, and no matter how many times he'd been forced to do this, whether it was friend or stranger, it wasn't easy. He supposed if it got too easy, he would know he had become too desensitized to death, immune to caring. The boots he took off first and tied to the pack. They were still in decent condition and would no doubt be needed badly back at the compound; shoes were always in the biggest demand as decent shoes or boots were so hard to produce. The man's belt also went into the pack, but the jacket was ruined along with the pants. As he went to roll him over, Dylan felt something in the pants pocket. He reached in and pulled out a folded up piece of paper; judging by its condition, it was fairly new.

"Matt, hey, Matt, check this out, he had it in his pocket."

"This is a notice to all Wilders, Wanderers, and Citizens. We, the United Front Party, are calling all to notice that we have begun rebuilding a protected, safe, and secure community in the abandoned city of Fontana, beside Lake Dakota. The U.F.P. invites all who are willing to become part of this community to come in and be taken care of. We, the U.F.P., are also prepared to defend our citizens with extreme force; don't mistake our kindness for weakness. U.F.P."

Matt softly whistled before he spoke. "This could change everything, Dylan."

Dylan nodded and was already thinking that as much as he disliked it, he had to get back to the compound and call a meeting of the council as soon as possible. This was something they would have to speak about; decisions would need to be made.

"Okay, Matt, let's grab what we can and head back

across the highway. I would like to be at least two or three miles away from here before dusk. It's not safe around here with this meat and those gunshots; we better fill our water bottles while we still can. I want to get an early start tomorrow. The council will definitely want to hear about this and discuss what actions we will all need to take." Matt nodded, and they both started to gather all the things as quickly as possible. Nothing important would be left for others to find, then they both headed off to the tree line.

CHAPTER 5

Max Jackson was not a happy man. He was, at this moment in time, furious. Things had been going so well up to now, and he just couldn't believe it had turned to crap so goddamned quickly. He was pacing up and down his office trying to work out where things had gone wrong and what he could do to get them back on track. Max was the official leader of the United Front Party and had been for the last two years. What started as one of the many scattered survivors' colonies had been built up over the last three or four years into one of the top four groups in this area of the country, all trying to establish themselves as the only legitimate government party.

"Goddamn it, Ricer. I mean really, what the hell is going on out there?" Max didn't give Ricer, his Armed Response Leader, a chance to reply.

"I mean, you were supposed to be doing a non-aggressive patrol on the northern sector, now, NOW! I have three people in body bags in my lobby, and nine people in the hospital, two of whom will be lucky if they even see tomorrow at this rate!" Max exploded.

"Sir, if you let me explain, it wasn't my fault. The League ambushed us," Ricer replied with a shake of his head. The last place he wanted to be right now was standing in front of Max while he had one of his legendary rages.

The League, or Populist Action League as they were officially called, was one of the four big groups all vying for power in the northern sector. The P.A.L. was a very militarized group with an aggressive approach to all things, and also a very rigid chain of command and military-style community. They were, at this point, the U.F.P.'s biggest problem, one they had been trying to handle diplomatically, and failing, for perhaps the last two years.

"Ricer, you are in charge of patrols, you were leading that patrol, and so what happens is your fault! I don't want excuses; I want results! And what I don't want is dead citizens in my goddamn building!" Max shouted.

"Listen to me, Ricer; I know you have a tough job, I've been there, too, remember? But, I put you in charge because I know you're up to it." Max sighed, rubbing his hands through what was left of his hair.

It really wasn't Ricer's fault. These things happened, but lately he just couldn't help but let his temper get the best of him.

"Look, I didn't mean to shout, I'm just frustrated is all. The P.A.L., up to this point, won't even try to settle things without blood loss, and, if anything, reports suggest they are stepping things up. We need to take on a more defensive position and start to gather some more people. The P.A.L. is in a really strong position to our North but weak to our South and East." Max was pointing to a map hanging on his wall as he spoke, the entire thing covered with red marks and symbols.

"You want to build up the strength to our North in a holding position, and send out patrols South and East to try to bring in more people? Right?" Ricer was pretty sure he knew that's what Max was going to say; he'd been doing this all his life, first as a police officer and then later in the military.

"Yes, Ricer, we need to grow, not just in our overall position on the map, but also with people. The more people we have, the better our position as a legitimate government will be," Max replied.

As Max started to go over what he'd been thinking, they moved to a large table which was covered by another map. This map had small models which represented their borders and positions. Max pointed to several of the circled places with his finger.

"Those circles all mark different communities and compounds we have either confirmed or heard rumors about. We need to get those people to join us. I'm not forcing them to, but I want them with us, not going over to the P.A.L. because no one ever bothered to ask them."

"Sir, I think if we take an oversized patrol, perhaps double the regular troops, we can be prepared for whatever happens. Maybe offer to take members of individual groups back to the capital to show them what we are all about here; what we are trying to achieve." Ricer suggested. He had done this on several occasions previously; the plan had worked quite well. Let the people see what they would be joining, let them know the U.F.P. could be trusted, and their people would be cared for. People needed to know they were safe, and this community could really benefit all of them.

Max thought about it while he studied the large map;

the idea was good. Ricer was a good man, he'd done this sort of thing before, but that wasn't what was troubling him. He wanted to send out enough men to be able to deal with any threats, but too many would only intimidate the people he was trying to entice.

"Okay, do it, Ricer, double squad, hand-picked by you, and I want you humping double medical supplies and rations. Some of those people out there will need them, and a little goodwill goes a long way."

"Yes, sir. I'll get started right away, head out at 0600 tomorrow morning." Ricer touched his knuckles to his head as he walked out. No drinks for him tonight, now he had too much to organize. There was always something, he thought to himself, as he laughed and walked out. Max was worried, but what else was new, he thought, as he shook his head. He would give himself more than an ulcer if he didn't start to take it easy, but what choice did he have? Someone had to be in charge, and, now, it appeared there was no other option than for that person to be him.

CHAPTER 6

Dylan and Matt headed out early; they wanted to get as far away from here as they could before daylight set in. Besides, cold breakfast and cold weather didn't exactly make lying in their sleeping bags that appealing a prospect. They were lugging a bit more gear than when they had set off, so the early start wouldn't hurt, and would give them a bit more flexibility on the way back. Neither of them said much to each other; both of them were deep in thought about the notice which they had found in that stranger's pocket. All of the people back in the compound knew there were new governments forming; they had all heard the whispers and stories from people passing through, but nothing definite, nothing like this before. Once Cinam2 had reached to almost all parts of the world, the government had tried some drastic measures, none effective. These measures hurt more than they ever helped. Desperate times called for desperate measures. It had started with camps for the so-called infected people; that had been a useless gesture, and then there were more horrific measures. Death squads, the army or mercenaries employed by the government, had begun to exterminate people. It started off slowly, a house here or a house there, but then it turned into a couple of houses. By the time the government realized the death squads were out of control, they were killing whole towns, women, children, and animals. They killed everyone; it didn't matter if they were sick or not. These groups were out of control and even the army battled them in the streets.

In the end, it meant nothing and helped even less, killing the few people who could have survived otherwise. By this stage, any sense of order had completely broken down. Some of these groups, those not ravaged by the virus, moved into towns the government and other groups had already cleaned out, and began to set up bases, establishing their own small, brutal forms of governments. Dylan and Matt didn't know if it was one of these groups who had made that flyer, or one of the other groups rumored to be out there trying to help restore order, but either way they intended to find out. It was almost mid-afternoon when Dylan and Matt made the approach to the compound, both of them dog-tired and weary, looking forward to a hot shower and a hot meal. Matt gave the double whistle, and they both stood up a little to see who was on the wall. It didn't pay to walk straight in, no matter how quiet things had been; a lot could change in twenty-four hours these days. It was Frank who waved them in and shouted down for the gates to be opened. Not the main gate, just a small gate set off to one side. Originally, the big double gates had been designed to let vehicles enter and exit, but fuel was so rare these days, it hadn't been opened in years.

"Hey, Dylan, I'm going to put that bear skin out to cure and then head over to the showers to wash up. I'll be back in half an hour or so, okay?" Matt asked over his shoulder. He wasn't waiting for an answer; he was already halfway up the compound.

Dylan just shook his head and laughed. He knew why Matt was going to wash up; he did a lot more washing these days! Brea, his sister, had definitely gotten his best friend's attention. He'd thought a lot about the two of them, and to be honest to himself, he couldn't think of another man he would rather have by his side or his sister's. As he headed toward the compounds armory to add the weapons they had found with the stranger, he looked around the compound and noticed, not for the first time, just how crowded it had become. Over the last few years, people around the compound had settled into a comfortable routine, you could say, not easy by any means, but things had definitely been easier on them than the beginning. They had all maybe gotten a little complacent. He'd been reflecting a lot lately on what had happened and what they all had become. He needed something to change, he wanted it to; there just had to be something better than this for his friends and family. He put the notice in his pocket and his second stop after the armory would be to the council meeting room to call a general meeting. There had to be something better out there for them, and it was time for a change. As Dylan walked into the outer room he could see the lights on in the main room, so he knew someone was there, probably Anthony, he seemed to live in this room!

"Ah, Dylan, how nice of you to grace us with your presence at last." Anthony chuckled to himself. Dylan just shook his head and frowned at him. He really was a pain in the ass, but the man did a good job for the compound, and no matter how much Dylan disliked him, he was glad he was part of the council.

"No problems, Anthony, you know me; I'm always happy to help out." Which they both knew was a lie, but neither could be bothered to argue about it. They had both been over this before, and nothing would change.

"I found something interesting out there, Anthony, something important. I want the council called as soon as possible; I think we all need to hear about this and we have to plan what we are going to do." Anthony just nodded, despite all their differences, he knew when Dylan was worried about something, and if he was worried, then they should all be worried.

"I'll go around to all of the houses now and let them all know that we are calling a general assembly. What is it that you have found, Dylan?" Dylan didn't bother to read the note to him he just passed it over for Anthony to read for himself.

As he sat and watched Anthony read the notice he hoped this could be the change he thought they all needed, something good, finally, something better for his sister and brother. Anthony just shook his head as he read; he rubbed his eyes and read the notice once again, just to make sure he understood it completely.

"This could be good or bad, but you already know this, I can see it in your eyes, Dylan. Is it good or bad in your opinion? What are you thinking? Never mind, save it for the meeting. I'll go and let everyone know, and we will all meet back here in the morning. Go home, see your family, and get cleaned up; have something to eat before you waste away." Anthony told him with a look of concern.

"Sure, that would be good; I'll see you and the council back here in the morning," Dylan replied.

Dylan nodded to Anthony, pushed his chair in quietly and walked out. He was actually pretty damn hungry, and his sister always had something ready for him, especially if he'd been out overnight.

Dylan walked into the house quietly; he wanted to grab a shower before he started explaining everything that had happened.

As Dylan turned off the taps in the shower, he could hear voices and laughter coming from the living room; Matt had shown up, and he could also smell something pretty damn good, too. He hadn't realized how hungry he was until now, and his stomach started rumbling just to prove a point. He threw on jeans and a top and headed towards the kitchen. He was always thankful for what his sister had managed to achieve around the house with so little; it always made him smile whenever he was home. Let's be honest; there hadn't been a lot to smile about over the last decade.

"There he is! At least I think it's him; you don't smell like a dump, so it's hard to be sure." Matt ducked a playful swipe to the head as he chuckled away.

"You weren't so pretty yourself, blossom, and I see you've managed to find yourself something to eat already," Dylan replied as he sat down, sliding his plate over towards himself. "As usual, seems like I'm the last one to get anything to eat around this joint," Dylan said, tormenting his sister.

"If we all waited for you to eat, we'd be dead and buried by now, Dylan! Besides, Matt and Seb were hungry, dinner was ready, and so we decided to start without you," Brea replied curtly. She knew he was only teasing her, but as usual, she took the bait hook, line, and sinker. She was always complaining he let her cooking get ruined because it was cold before he finally sat down to eat.

"I had to let the council know about that notice we found, then drop off some weapons to the armory on the way back. Couldn't be helped, sorry. Dinner is lovely by the way." Dylan wasn't really worried about his sister's grumpy mood; she was always like this after he'd been away a few days. The stress and anxiety worrying about them while they were away had to go somewhere, so when they finally made it back, she was already worn out and relieved that everyone was back safe.

"Matt told Seb and me about the notice that you found. Do you think there could really be a new government starting up, a real one? What we have here is great, but to be involved in something bigger where we could all sleep a little easier at night would be good." Brea asked with just a little bit of hope creeping into her voice.

"I'm not sure, sis, it would be nice to stop looking over our shoulders so much, but we have been out here a long time now looking after ourselves; it would be hard to get everyone excited to change. Besides that, we have to be careful about what sort of people this U.F.P. group is; I'd want to have a good look at what they had got set up before I moved our people to them," Dylan said.

"I agree with Dylan on this one, Brea, we have to take this very slowly; we can't rush into this. It has taken us so long to get where we are and I'm not willing to throw it all away." Matt had a determined look set on his face they had all seen many times before. They all continued to eat the rest of their meals, contemplating what the future held for all of them and hoping for once things would work out in their favor. As Dylan and Matt helped clean the dishes, while Seb and Brea both wiped them and put them away, Dylan couldn't help but smile and think how lucky he was to have them all with him, a smaller family since disaster struck, but a family nevertheless. As he got undressed and lay down to sleep, Dylan started thinking about the U.F.P. notice they'd found and what the council would think about it. Eventually, they would need to become part of the world again and that would mean taking the first step. Maybe that first step would have to be a blind leap of faith, but, either way, something had to change.

They were all up early, fed, and dressed, ready to head over to the council meeting that was being organized for this morning, and which would most likely run all day. No one wanted to be late; they had a lot to discuss. They all filed into the council meeting room, Dylan and Matt headed up to the big table at the front of the room while Brea and Seb sat down in the chairs placed along either wall. They all nodded and said small greetings to one another as they moved through the people. It looked like almost everyone was there already, except those on guard duty around the compound. Anthony called the meeting to order, and everyone stopped the small conversations they were having and waited to listen.

"Okay, now that everyone is here, I would like to cut straight to the point. We've all read a copy of the notice Dylan and Matt found, and I've placed a few copies around the room for anyone who hasn't had the opportunity to read it yet. This is a big decision for us all, as individuals, families, and also as a community. I want to hear everyone's opinions, no matter how they feel, negative or positive. I'm going to start with my own and move around to my left, giving everyone at the table a chance to speak as the representative of their family. So far over the last ten years, our small community has managed to survive here relatively well, especially the last five years. We have overcome so much and worked so hard to gather what we have, that no matter what, we have to tread very carefully before we rush into making any decisions. We have survived, we are surviving, and we could survive for another ten, twenty, or even fifty years, but surviving isn't living, and it won't help our kids to live either. We need to grow and become part of something bigger than just here. I vote we give this new group a chance to see what and who they are." Anthony finished speaking and looked around at the heads of the families before sitting down.

Several more council representatives said very much the same thing over the next few hours, some slightly different, but in effect the same message. Dylan took his turn to stand and speak. He was the last one and agreed with most of the other council leaders that they needed to grow and prosper to live. Surviving to an old age just to die off slowly wasn't an option anymore. They all agreed to organize a few people to head out and gather what intelligence they could about the U.F.P. Find out whom and what they were, and prepare the compound for whatever needed to be done.

"Dylan and Matt, I think I speak for everyone when I say we think it's best if you two head out and find out exactly what it is that this group is all about. We trust you both with our futures, and we wish you all the best of luck. Godspeed and good weather to both of you, and we will await your return," Anthony said to both of them as he addressed the whole room.

"I think I speak for both of us when I say we would be happy to do this for you all, and honestly, I wouldn't want to send anyone out to risk their lives unless I was going with them. Matt and I will do our absolute best to ensure the safety of all of you; we consider you both our friends and our extended families," Dylan spoke to the whole room.

"Yup, what he said." Matt chimed in with a chuckle.

"And besides, we all know that he needs someone to hold his hand so he won't get lost!" Matt punched his friend in the arm and ducked a punch in return. They both shook everyone's hands as people filed out and accepted small gifts of luck, while others offered to pop in for a quick meal before they left and to make sure Seb and Brea were looked after while they were gone.

CHAPTER 7

Ricer was moving his patrol at a fairly decent pace through the forest. They had been on the move now for almost three days, and he was hoping to travel the next three at an even better pace now that they'd all settled into a routine. The country they had been passing through up until now had provided fairly decent game and a good amount of cover. Most of the men and women had been hunting as they moved so they hadn't had to dip into their rations at all, which meant they would be able to patrol further out into the countryside. They had another four or five days to go before they reached the edge of what they considered their territory. After that, it was all bandit country, wild and untamed, but no other groups were approaching from this direction so they shouldn't encounter too much open hostility. With a group the size of the patrol he was leading, Wilders wouldn't be a problem; only other large groups would openly attack him. The small communities would defend themselves, but most of these weren't overly aggressive; they were normally positioned defensively, which meant they weren't keen to leave whatever defensive position they had established to attack someone, let alone a group this big. Ricer was hoping they would be out no longer than thirty days or so, most of his patrol members had families back in the city, and they tended to lose concentration after more than thirty days on patrol. There were forty members in his patrol, double the usual twenty in the squads they patrolled with, so he had plenty of firepower and plenty of people to carry supplies and scout with. The only problem so far was his two squad leaders hated each other with a passion. It was so bad Ricer almost had to stop an argument from coming to blows the night before. Both squad leaders were exceptionally talented and great at what they did, but there was a reason they were squad leaders, they didn't play well with others, and they didn't like taking orders from other people. Ricer just had to laugh; it was better than crying at this point! It was bad enough they had to put up with him on their patrol, but now they had the other squad leader treading on their toes, too!

If Brent and Jess spent as much time and energy on patrolling as they did on trying to make Ricer's life hell, then he swore they would be twice as far along as they were now and he wouldn't have this damn constant earache. Both were ex-military, but both had had to climb very different career ladders over their lifetimes, which was the biggest thing that kept them at each other's throats.

Brent's dad and granddad had both been military; most of his family had been born, raised and fed military from a very young age. He didn't wonder what he was going to be when he grew up. He knew he was going to be general; the only thing he didn't know was how young or old he'd be when he achieved it.

Jess, on the other hand, came from a very poor,

uneducated background, and she'd had to drag herself out by the fingernails, no easy steps here. She'd had to fight family, friends, environment, and even the very ingrained military traditions to get where she had in the military. She resented what she thought was Brent's fast track through the military, and he, as far as Ricer could tell, resented everything about her and where she came from.

Ricer would break the pair of them before they returned if it was the last thing he did! Together they were great squad leaders. He wouldn't have picked them if he didn't trust them with his life, but this childish bickering had to stop before he cracked both their heads together.

"Jess, Brent, get your mangy asses over here stat," he shouted. Both were in separate camps with their groups, and he wanted everyone to fight like a unit and less like two squads. It might just save their lives one day.

"As of tomorrow, I want both of your squads to be camping in the same area. I want them eating, sleeping, and crapping together, and that includes the two of you! Got it?" They both nodded, but the looks they gave him would probably strip paint off a car.

"Okay, I want both of your point men to take the lead at the same time from now on; they all need to learn the habits of those around them. I want this patrol to be a single being, with one brain—that brain will be me—everything under the brain will do as I damn tell it to! Comprende, mi amigos?" Two very quick "yes, sirs" echoed across the camp, and Ricer dismissed them both with a nod.

It felt much bloody better to get that off his chest, and a little screaming never hurt anyone at all. He allowed himself a small chuckle as he wandered around the perimeter of his camp to check on the security he had out. Just one last look before he slept. Maybe they could pull it off, after all. Hell, those two would never be best friends, but once they got over their own pride and stubbornness, they would be damn good leaders and more than a force to be reckoned with. This growing community of theirs could never have too many leaders.

The entire group rose early the next morning, well before sunset. Ricer was pushing them as hard as he dared, to get the most out of them; he wouldn't break them, but he'd damned well go as close to as it as possible.

It was a cloudy day and getting colder, probably rain, but not cold enough for snow, yet. This time of the year, with winter fast approaching, they were all wearing extra cold-weather gear, and they each carried parts of a tent between two or three people. This way they could spread the load and they all had somewhere slightly warmer to sleep. Over the summer months, they most likely would be happy to sleep under the stars, saving carrying the extra weight. With the temperature fast dropping, it wouldn't be long before they were all run down and sick. Ricer didn't need to deal with that as well as the rest of the things on his mind.

They were all making good time when he called a halt at a small stream and told them all to get some chow and take a thirty-minute break. Ricer asked one of his runners to call in the scouts and both the squad leaders so that they could have a briefing while the group rested. He also wanted to get a report on progress from the scouts.

The two scouts didn't have anything major to report, just some old hunting signs, and no fresh signs of any people. They were still fairly close to their main town, so they hadn't expected to see much until at least a week's march out from the city. Ricer's two squad leaders both agreed, which was a bloody miracle, he thought, on a map position they both thought would be an achievable goal by last light. He was happy with how they were pushing their men to gain a little bit each day.

The scouts moved back out into their lead positions. After everyone had some food, they all cleaned up the area as much as possible and headed out again. It was hard to cover up the fact that there was a large group moving through the area, but they wanted to leave as little clues as possible about the size of their group.

The group reached the hill they had all agreed on at lunch was a good finishing point for the day's march. They had done it thirty minutes quicker than Ricer had expected them to, and he called a halt for the day. This high point would be an easily defensible position, not that he was overly worried at this point, but it was always better to be safe rather than sorry. After all, it was his responsibility to look after the safety and well-being of all those who were under his command. He called his two squad leaders in once they had their men organized and asked the two scouts to come in, too.

"Okay, I'm pretty happy with the progress so far, people. Just be sure to keep an eye on your people's fatigue levels each night after chow. Have a couple of senior people go around and check for any injuries and make sure that they are checking their boots and socks, as well. I don't want to lose someone because of a rubbish pair of boots or wet socks. Right, see to your people. We will be on the move at the same time in the morning. Good job, people, let's keep it up." Ricer finished speaking and started looking at the few old maps he'd managed to get his hands on.

The two scouts knuckled their heads and started to head off to where they would be camped out for the night. It was about six hundred feet or so further forward than the main camp. They acted as a forward observation point, and it gave them an early head start when the main camp moved out in the morning.

"Jess, Brent, wait a minute, please. Good job today, I want to see if we can squeeze them all just a little bit more tomorrow, wring the most out of them before the weather chooses to dump itself all over us. Don't break them, just keep them going at the same pace you have, okay?"

"Yes, sir," they both replied.

"Okay, you're both dismissed for the night, keep up the good work." Ricer knuckled his head, and the two squad leaders knuckled back before they strode away towards the food lines and their people's tents to see to their duties.

He would wait until all his people had been fed and the camp started to quiet down, and then he'd make his rounds for the night and check all his sentries. It wouldn't take him long and he liked to take the opportunity to talk with all the men and women to see how they were feeling. It was a good way to gauge the general happiness among those around the camp. After that, he'd turn in for a few hours, but he'd be up again around 1:00 a.m. to check on the change of sentries. Then a couple more hours sleep before waking to see what the next day had delivered for them.

CHAPTER 8

Matt and Dylan had been making good time and distance. For the first week, they had been traveling in a northerly direction across the more familiar areas around the compound; the problem now was they were reaching less familiar territory. Last night they'd decided to hold up in a deserted house because it was getting close to dark. Neither had been this far north before; both would have to be extra diligent in keeping an eye on their surroundings as they traveled.

The pre-dawn morning light creeping over the horizon gave the two of them just enough light to make something quick to eat, clean up around where they'd been staying, and make a move. It always paid to act as if someone was tracking you, leaving them as little information as possible to go on was always the safest way to move around a hostile area. Both were wearing their heavier winter clothes now, even though it hadn't snowed yet. They would probably throw them in their packs later on during the day as they both warmed up. They had seen quite a bit of wildlife as they had been moving, which was a good sign. It indicated to them that there weren't a lot of people hunting in this area, and that meant that they wouldn't have to deal with a large group of people. That they hadn't actually seen anyone at all yet was another good sign, and there weren't a lot of abandoned buildings around either. Normally, people liked to settle into bigger places where it was easier to start again with buildings and amenities that were already constructed, and those structures were easier to defend and easier to improve.

After the breakdown of the government, and the larger bombings and massacres had stopped, a lot of areas had simply been left abandoned. One morning families were sitting and eating their breakfast, and the next, nothing; everyone was gone. With the virus spreading through communities very quickly, everyone generally tended to start showing symptoms at the same time. The young, the old, and the weak always died first, but the healthy, unless they were immune, died quickly after. It didn't matter if you were the fittest, healthiest athlete in town; the virus soon put an end to that. If no one had been left to clean up after they died, then the corpses of those that had passed away were normally left in beds or rooms of the houses or the hospitals where they had died.

Ten years later there wasn't a lot left to be sickened by. The smell was long since gone, and the flesh rotted away or eaten by scavengers. Both Dylan and Matt had gone through this too many times to count, sometimes even with people they knew. Now, they had long since stopped worrying about the skeletons left to stand guard over their former wards.

The first six to twelve months after the virus swept through had been the worst by far. No one liked going into cars or houses then, with their sickly sweet smell of rotting flesh and death soaked into every surface of the building.

Matt called a halt about midafternoon, having spotted a small group of houses about two miles distant, most likely a small town, as they had both emerged from a small copse of trees. Leaving the safety of the forest always made Dylan wary. The forest was their safe place. They could run and hide, and disappear if they needed to; the forest meant life.

"Let's wait up here, Dylan; we can both grab a bite to eat and drink. I haven't seen anything moving down there but I'd like to give it another hour or so, just to make sure." Matt was looking through his small pair of binoculars while he spoke softly. They were one of his prized possessions. He hadn't shown up with a lot, but those binoculars had saved both of their asses a few times over the years.

"Okay, sure. Is there any way we can go around them, just avoid this area altogether by skirting along the edge of the forest for a few more days?" Dylan would always rather avoid taking any unnecessary chances, if possible, but, at the moment, time was too crucial. It wasn't the best scenario, but their safety would have to come in a close second to time.

"No. If you look to the left, there's a deep valley which I am pretty sure will have a river running through it at this time of the year. Then, to the right, there's that huge goddamn mountain. I would rather not walk up, over, or all the way around that damn mountain." Matt shook his head and took another look at the small town.

"Yep, the town will be the easiest, I think, even though I know that going into any town sucks. Going around will cost us at least three or four days, minimum. What do you think?" Matt asked.

"Okay, I'd rather not waste that much time either; this will get cold enough before we arrive anywhere. We will wait out an hour or so and then move down into the town. You can go first; I'll give you a ten-minute lead and then I'll follow you in and cover you. Head to that large white building first and then move to the right, sound good?" Dylan was sketching a diagram into the ground with a stick as he spoke. Matt nodded and kept scanning the town through his binoculars. He was marking all the different buildings and possible ambush points in his mind. He wanted to know exactly where he was for the next cover spot, and where Dylan would be as they moved through the town.

After they had finished eating and packed their kit away, they were ready to head out. Neither spoke, Dylan just slapped Matt on the back as he headed off and took up his bow and crouched ready to move out. He also reached into the holster near his ankle and checked that the 9mm pistol was secure, and the safety was on. There wasn't a lot of use spending all this time being careful and scouting out the place if the pistol fell out and fired off a round as they moved into position. Both Matt and he had their usual bows but had also brought the two 9 mm pistols along for added protection. Matt had wanted to bring a rifle as well, but at the last minute had decided the weight of the weapon was just too much for him as they were already carrying much more than they usually would.

Matt was halfway to the buildings now. As Dylan started to move out, he kept his eyes on Matt as much as possible to track the way Matt had taken, so there would only be one set of tracks leading in and it would be easier to follow them back out if anything went wrong and they had to fall back quickly. Matt had made it to the large white building. Dylan had stopped where he was behind a large tree so he could observe what Matt was up to, making sure that he was alright. Matt had moved to both sides of the building now, as far as possible without anyone further into the town being able to see him. He then moved back to the rear of the large building and was signaling Dylan to come down. Dylan moved off and headed down to where his friend was, still wary and scanning around just to make sure nothing had changed. It never paid to let your guard down, especially in strange areas where you were the trespasser.

"It's all boarded up and dusty inside from what I could see. I had a quick look along toward those other buildings; they all look the same from here. I couldn't see much signs of anyone living here recently; the entire place looks as if it has been picked clean. I'd say at some point people have been through here, but I don't think they stuck around any longer than it took to clean out the place," Matt whispered to Dylan under his breath.

"Okay, well, let's do a lap of the buildings. We'll cover each other, and then leapfrog from one to the next and make sure they're all closed up and empty. Better to be safe than sorry, I'd hate to bump into any surprises." Dylan was already up and moving to the first building as he finished speaking.

Matt just chuckled quietly and slowly stood up ready to cover his friend. They both took turns moving from building to building, doing a circle of each one, before moving on to the next. It was a painfully slow process, but it was better than assuming the place was empty and then having their throats slit in the night as they slept.

All total, it took almost two more hours before they were back at their starting point at the white building where they had first entered the town.

"We might as well hold up here for the rest of the day. It will be dark in two hours anyway and that will give us a chance to poke around and see what we can find. This building has that upstairs window; it would make a good vantage point. We could break off a board, and it will give us a good place to keep an eye on things," Dylan said. "Sure, sounds good. I want to have a good look inside that old hunting store, but the rest of the buildings look pretty well picked clean. I'll head over, check it out, and then I'll see you back here in probably an hour. Okay?" Matt asked.

"Yep, no worries. I'll see you back here in an hour. Be safe, okay? I'll break in through this cellar window and prop the boards up the way they were. No one will be able to tell any different, just in case anyone does come looking around," Dylan replied.

Matt nodded to his friend and then headed off in a large circle towards the hunting store that they had seen earlier.

Dylan took off his pack and pulled out a large pry bar and laid it to one side. He also wrapped up his jacket and slid it into his pack at the same time; all that scouting around had gotten him warmed up, and he'd be inside soon anyway. Besides that, it was his best jacket, and he didn't want to tear it breaking in through the window. He moved his pack off to one side underneath a bush, and then dropped down into the area where the basement window had been roughly boarded up as if it was only temporary and the occupants would soon be back.

They wouldn't be back and no one else had been either. So many people at the start believed that they would soon be back, but never made it out of the hospital or the camps; some didn't even make it that far. It took quite a bit to pry off that first board, but once he had it off and could get a bit more leverage, the rest came off easily. Within ten minutes he had pulled enough boards away to be able to slide in through the gap. It was pitch-black in the basement; it took a while for his eyes to adjust to the darkness. The air coming out through the hole he'd made smelled old and rotten; it was pretty obvious nothing had been down there in quite some time.

Dylan pulled a small wind-up LED penlight out of his pocket and started to wind it quickly. He shone it around the basement. He then tied a bandanna around his mouth and nose and dropped feet first down into the basement. He quickly worked the beam of the small torch around the dark basement and located the stairs leading up from the basement into the main part of the house; at least they were concrete and he wouldn't have to worry about falling through them.

A couple of years back, Matt and he had been checking an abandoned house, and he'd fallen through a set of rotten basement stairs. Dylan had been stuck there for over two hours until his friend had come back looking for him. The only thing he had hurt had been his pride, but Matt still teased him about the day that he'd "rescued him" from the scary stairs monster. Dylan smiled to himself and chuckled, never again would he walk up a set of stairs without checking them first to make sure they weren't bloody rotten! He switched off the torch as he slowly pushed the door open into the main level of the house. The heavy old thing was damn hard to push, over the years the hinges had closed up, another good sign no one had been around here anytime recently. As he looked around, he could see a fine layer of dust over everything and what was pushed into the corner almost made him do a double-take. He slowly shook his head as he recognized what was sticking out from the pile of blankets. He'd seen it too many times before. A pile of human remains would be what was under those rotted blankets.

Many times people had entered the homes of the sick after they died, gathering remains into a corner and then boarding up the houses in a futile attempt at stopping the virus from spreading. Dylan moved away from that corner. He didn't need to look at that, and he didn't need to add an image to his already big list of horrific things which he dreamt of during the night.

The kitchen and living rooms to his left looked empty; most of the drawers and cupboards were either open or smashed and lying scattered around the place. He moved up the stairs slowly placing one foot at a time onto each stair, sticking to the edge closest to the wall where the boards were strongest.

The next floor of the house didn't have much in it either, empty bedrooms with some rubbish and smashed furniture littering the floor and boarded-up windows as the other levels. At least with more windows, it was letting in a little bit of light, and he didn't have to keep winding the small torch. The small torches were rare, and he was afraid that one day it just wouldn't have another wind left in it.

The top level contained only one bedroom, but it had three separate windows which would give them a good view over most of the small town. Best of all it had an old mattress which looked okay to sleep on. Dylan carefully pried a board off each of the windows, then hammered it back into place, leaving a small gap that they could see out of, but from a distance wouldn't look any different from any of the other house windows. After he'd done the same to all the windows, he made his way back down through the house making sure they had a clear path all the way down to the basement in case they had to get in or out in a hurry. If anything went wrong, this would be a last resort because it would leave them trapped, without any way of being rescued. At least out in the town or the woods they would have a decent chance of escaping.

He grabbed his pack and pushed it down into the basement making sure not to tear it on anything, then climbed in afterward and headed back up to the top room to see if he could keep an eye on Matt and see what he was up to. It was fifteen minutes before he spotted Matt moving back around the small red house in his direction. Matt was pausing along the way to make sure he wasn't being watched. He lost sight of him a few minutes later; it was a couple of minutes before he heard three quick, sharp knocks come from the direction of the back of the house. Dylan knocked three times in reply and then he could hear small creaks as his friend made his way from the basement up to the upstairs room.

"Hey, Dylan, nice place you got here!" Matt chuckled as he threw himself down on the old mattress shrugging off his pack and made himself comfortable.

"Ha, yeah, I know, right, it's no Hilton, and the room service is terrible, but it beats sleeping in the cold outside, and I got it pretty cheap, huh?" Dylan shot back.

They both laughed and punched each other on the shoulders before getting themselves under control. It was always amazing to Dylan how the tension could be pushed aside for a few fun moments, no matter how bad things were.

"I didn't find much of anything, Dylan; that place had been well and truly cleaned up a long time ago. What was surprising is I got about forty rounds of 9mm ammunition off the floor where a box had broken open, and the people had obviously been in too much of a hurry to stick around and pick them up. Hmm, what else, oh yeah, I found a decent skinning knife kicked under a pile of rubbish and probably the best of all, a box of arrowheads and two boxes of shafts." Matt was smirking as he said the last bit. Dylan shot him a dirty look.

"Not much, huh! You're a smart ass! Matt, those bloody arrowheads and shafts are priceless, not that the ones we make are rubbish, but those machined ones are perfect!" Dylan was smiling now.

"I thought you'd like that. Obviously, when they cleaned the place out the first few times, they weren't that interested in that sort of thing. The other things will be useful too, and I don't mind carrying the extra weight, I've got a little bit of room," Matt said.

"Okay, nice work, man. Let's make something to eat and drink, and then get some rest okay? I want to move out of here early before first light so that we'll be well into those trees to the north. I'll take first watch while you grab some sleep, and then I'll wake you when I get tired." Matt nodded and started to make them up a cold drink and something to eat, while Dylan tidied up their gear and settled in a chair where he could see out one of the windows.

It would be a quiet night, with a little luck, and a lot warmer than where they'd both spent the last few nights out in the open with nothing but leaves or branches to give them some cover.

After spending an uneventful night in the upstairs of the white house, both of them were up and on their way well before the sun even started to show itself over the mountain. They would push hard today to make up for not covering much distance yesterday because of stopping in the town. Besides that, they wanted to be wherever it was that they had to be before winter closed in too much and the thick snow made their lives even more difficult.

They were setting a pretty good pace when Dylan heard a dull cracking sound up ahead and then a small shout, quickly cut off by Matt. He dropped into cover instantly to the side of the trail they'd been moving along, and knocked an arrow up to his bow, his eyes quickly scanning around him in a circle. Dylan heard Matt give three quick whistles which meant that he was okay and to move up. Dylan double-timed it up the track to find his friend off to one side with his foot caught in some sort of old steel animal trap. He quickly pulled out his knife and together they pried open the jaws of the trap and Matt pulled his foot out before the trap banged shut.

"I'm sorry, crap. I didn't see the bloody thing until the last second as my foot went down on it. I tried to throw myself to one side, but it still managed to grab me on the end of my boot." Matt looked more embarrassed than hurt.

"That's okay; it could be a lot worse," Dylan said as he stripped off his friend's boot and sock to see what damage the rusty steel teeth had done to his foot.

For the most part, the teeth had missed his foot, but his last two toes were bloody, and as he ran his fingers along them a sharp intake of breath from Matt let him know that one, if not both, were broken.

"The good news is you still have five little pigs, but the bad news is, two of those little pigs are bloody and probably broken. I don't suppose you have up-to-date medical insurance by any chance, sir?" They both laughed, and Matt shook his head.

"Okay, I'll clean them up and bandage them, then put some of that anti-bacteria powder we have left on them. Hopefully, if we can keep them clean, they won't get infected. There's not much we can do about the broken bones, they'll heal up slowly, but I'll strap them best I can, okay? Are you going to be able to keep going or should we head back for the compound?" Dylan asked.

"No way am I going back now, Dylan. We've gone too far, and I'll be okay. Stupid rookie mistake, treading on an old rabbit trap anyway. God knows how long the bloody thing has been sitting there waiting for some idiot to tread on it. Fix me up; you take the point and we'll keep moving until sunset, okay?" Matt had that determined look in his eyes, and Dylan knew better than to try and talk his friend out of it.

"Okay, Matt, but you whistle if you need to rest, and I'll keep dropping back to check on you." Matt nodded, but Dylan knew his friend was too bloody stubborn to whistle, so he would just have to force him to take it a little bit easier, no matter how much he grumbled about it and told him he was okay.

They packed away their gear and kept moving along the path. Twice more Dylan found old traps that had been set and forgotten; he triggered them with a stick and then tied them to his pack. He didn't like them, but they were useful, and you never knew when they might come in handy. The funniest part was when he gave Matt one to carry, a little jingling reminder of how dumb he was, maybe now they wouldn't all have to listen to that stupid stair story.

Their progress wasn't as quick now, but they were still making a good time up until sunset when they found a nice, thick patch of trees close to a stream where they could safely hold up until the next day. Matt went down and got some water and washed his foot so that Dylan could properly clean the wound again and then bandage it up for the night.

When he got back, Dylan had arranged their small camp and had a small fire going ready to boil some water to clean Matt's foot. They also had a hot meal for the first time in days. The thick woods and all the trees would dissipate the smoke, and also cover any of the light from their fire. Still, they would only have it lit long enough to cook their food and clean Matt's wounded foot, and then they would bury the ashes. After cleaning Matt's foot, they both had a chance to sit and eat the rough stew that Dylan had thrown together. It always amazed Dylan how much difference a hot meal could make when you were away from home and out in the cold. After clearing up, they both got comfortable, and Matt took his first watch so Dylan could grab some sleep. They had also rearranged the packs to put some of Matt's stuff into Dylan's pack so that he would be able to take it easier over the next few days. A little more weight in his pack wouldn't bother Dylan; the pace was the most important thing at this point of their journey.

"Hey Matt, I can't believe you trod on a rabbit trap! I think I might start calling you bugs bunny, huh!" Dylan started laughing himself silly as Matt gave him a not-so-gentle kick to the back of the head with his healthy foot.

"Yeah, wise guy, laugh it up. I suppose I deserve that after all these years of teasing you about the stairs, eh." Matt chuckled to himself as they both got comfortable. Dylan rolled over to grab some sleep. Bloody rabbit trap, Matt thought to himself; how stupid could he get! And Dylan wouldn't shut up about it, or let him forget about it, either.

CHAPTER 9

Since Matt and Dylan had left a week earlier, things around the compound had continued in the same way they normally did. Everyone had things to do. They had been doing the same things for so long now that most tasks had become second nature to all of them. There were people assigned to bake bread; others were in charge of drying out all the different sorts of meat the hunters brought in. The compound had very limited electricity. They didn't have the room for a massive array of solar panels—even if they could get them—so they made do with the ones they had.

The solar panels were arranged around the wall at the best vantage point to catch the sun coming through the forest around the compound. Wiring ran down from the panels into a room set off to one side. In the room, they had accumulated a large amount of batteries all wired together to produce a large cell which the solar panels could charge. They had very limited electricity for lights. Any appliances could only be used if essential and for the good of the whole compound, not just because an individual needed them for one reason or another.

They preserved a lot of the meat and any fruit or vegetables they managed to grow in the small plantations around the compound. They could either preserve it in jars or dry it out, and it would keep that way; meat was easy to rehydrate in a stew or could be eaten cold or dried as a jerky. Most of the hunters preferred the jerky so they could carry it while on the move since it didn't weigh as much.

Brea was normally happy to lend a hand wherever needed and hadn't been assigned to any one job in particular. Most of the time, she and Seb normally helped out in the gardens. Brea had always had a green thumb; it helped her deal with things to be able to work in the compound's garden. Occasionally, Seb would go out with the hunters or the scavengers if they weren't going out for more than a few hours. Brea's green thumb had proven very valuable to the compound; when it came to certain crops and plants, she could normally grow things when others had tried and failed. With most of the pre-prepared commercial seeds long since used, the compound had to gather seeds from the fruit and vegetables that they grew, cultivate them into seedlings, and transplant them. Initially, they had a lot of failures and the first few years had been very hard on them all.

The people in the compound hadn't necessarily been gardeners, cooks, hunters, tailors, electricians, etc., before the virus had swept through the country. They might have worked in offices, driven trucks, or even cleaned buildings, which meant all the different jobs they had around the compound had to be learned through trial and error. Sometimes a person might have a little experience in one area, so that automatically made them an expert compared to the others who knew nothing. When the Cinam2x Virus swept through the world, it wasn't worried about who it killed, who survived, what they did before, or what they would have to do afterward. It just killed and killed, gardeners or scientists; it didn't care.

CHAPTER 10

Dylan and Matt lay together under the hedge where they had dived for cover, even trying not to breathe, as the small group of men moved slowly past them. The fact that they had almost walked straight into the other group's camp just showed Dylan that they were experienced woodsman. The only thing that had saved both their asses was the fact that the two of them were even better.

They had been making damn good time up until this point. Maybe they were moving a little too quickly; mistakes got you killed.

Dylan looked over at Matt, who was making some persistent head movements, obviously trying to tell Dylan that they should try and crawl backward towards the trail they had just crossed. Dylan shook his head no. These guys would most likely cut their back trail at some point sooner or later; he was going to have to deal with them either way. Dylan motioned with his hand for Matt to just stay put and for him to be quiet. He was trying to think of the easiest and safest way to get them both out of this. He had counted at least five men moving around the camp, and from his position lying in the bushes, he could see only four of them had left. He turned his head to look at Matt and held up five fingers, then made a walking motion with his fingers and held up four fingers. Matt nodded and gave him the thumbs up sign that he agreed with Dylan's count, and he also made the classic gun signal with his hand. Dylan nodded at his friend; he'd seen the high-powered rifles each man was carrying, and they all looked very capable of using them. The men were all dressed in ex-military uniforms. They all seemed to have come from the same unit, originally, as most of the uniforms matched the others.

As far as he could tell, there was only one man left in the camp; the other four had left on a patrol or something. Dylan and Matt watched the one man move about the camp and from his limp they worked out why he'd been left in the camp and hadn't been taken out on the patrol with his buddies.

Matt moved over towards Dylan and whispered in his ear, "We need to move Dylan; one guy we can deal with, but five? There's no way even both of us together can get through five of these guys. Those rifles are serious, and they look like they know what they are doing with them. What are you thinking? Cross straight through their camp quiet as mice, and then if they find our trail it'll only lead them back to here?" Dylan nodded at his friend and started to plan the route that they'd take through the camp. This way he'd know where they were headed without having to think too much about it while they were on the move.

"Yeah, we'll give those guys another ten or fifteen minutes, then I want to cut straight through their camp," Dylan whispered back. "We can't afford to take them all on; we can't really even risk tangling with that one guy, limp or not. Who knows, they seem to be doing quite well out here, they could be left over from one of those death squads or ex-special forces who have been kicking around these forests for years." If they screwed this up, and he let loose with that rifle, they would have to be ready to put down some serious miles.

"Okay, well, I'll wait for you to make the first move, Dylan, and then I'll follow, okay?" Matt asked Dylan. Dylan just nodded at his friend and looked around the camp once more. All sounds of the other four men had faded away; the one with the limp who had been left behind was just tidying up what most likely were their breakfast things.

"Matt, in a few minutes we'll go, okay? Just stick close to me, but I want you covering me with your bow in case anything goes wrong. We can't afford for that guy to fire off a shot and warn the rest of his buddies that he's in trouble." Dylan was looking at the camp as he spoke; Matt was watching where those other four men had faded away into the forest opposite the camp.

"I know, Dylan; don't worry about it. I'll watch your back. Once you're clear, just make sure you're watching mine, buddy." Matt winked at his pal.

No matter how bad things got, Matt always had that damn silly smirk on his face. They were both looking at each other laying in the dirt and leaves; Matt smiling like a bloody escaped lunatic, and Dylan shaking his head at his crazy best friend.

The guy with the limp had finally settled down to some maintenance task of some sort and had his back to both of them. Dylan rose slowly into a crouch and started to clean leaves and small twigs away from in front of him. When he started to move, nothing would make any noises under his feet and give their position away.

As Dylan started moving through the trees, Matt stood slowly and moved silently toward a tree where he could cover Dylan's move across the camp, but not be seen by limp, in case the four men returned for some reason or other while they were making their move.

Dylan was already halfway there now, and he was almost level with the man with the limp, when he suddenly froze. He was staring away toward the opposite side of the camp where another man in camouflage had walked out of the trees.

Matt didn't even think, he swiveled and let loose his arrow with one fluid motion, his arrow taking the new guy cleanly through the throat as he was trying to bring his assault rifle up.

Matt and Dylan both had arrows up and covering the guy with the limp, but he must have thought the odds were in his favor, as he reached for the rifle at his side anyway. Both the arrows hit him at almost the same time, one through his throat and the other into his heart. He flew sideways out of his chair and was dead before he had even hit the ground.

"Damn. Damn it! Matt, where did that other guy come from? We could have made it." Dylan was shaking his head. They had watched for hours; that other guy must have been out of the camp the entire time, returning at probably the worst possible time.

"I don't know, Dylan, he must have been out before we even got here; it wasn't our fault. They would have killed us just as quickly; you know that." Matt was walking towards the first guy as he spoke. He wanted to remove his arrows and get the hell out of this camp before the rest of the men returned.

"I know, Matt, but with your limp and the two dead guys, those four who left this morning will be hard on our trails before the day is out. We need to clean up as quickly as possible and get the hell away from here!" Dylan was headed to the other body as he spoke over his shoulder. He would remove the arrow shafts, try to move the body, and make sure he left as little clues as possible for the men who would be returning.

"Hey, let's lay them on top of each other. Both of them have knives; we'll stick the knives into the arrow wounds and make it look as if they had a disagreement." Dylan was already trying to drag one of the men closer to the other as he spoke.

"Okay, but one thing. The arrows went all the way through; seriously, they would have had to have been up to their elbows to make stab wounds that deep," Matt replied.

"I know, it isn't perfect, but it could buy us some time, okay? You got anything better?" Dylan asked.

"Yeah, okay. Let's get this done and make a move," Matt replied, helping Dylan drag the dead men towards each other, and sticking their knives into each other. It wasn't perfect, but maybe, just maybe those two guys had hated each other anyway, who knows. They got their weird, macabre tableau sorted out as quickly as they could and got ready to get the hell out of Dodge.

"Well, Dylan, let's get a move on. I would like to get out of here and well on the way before their buddies get back!" Dylan agreed with him.

They both moved through the camp cleaning up their tracks and making it as hard as possible for the pursuit that would inevitably follow. Both Matt and Dylan were through the camp and on their way in less than ten minutes, trying to put as much distance as possible between them, the camp, and the two dead bodies they left behind.

They didn't stop to make anything for a meal after midday, just slowing to grab a drink and refill their bottles from a stream they had come across. Both of them were chewing some jerky to boost their energy.

It was almost complete darkness when they decided to hold up for the night—the sun long set over the mountains—and grab some much-needed rest. They hadn't put this much distance on in a single day since they had left the compound. Dylan thought about how far you could run when you could be being pursued by a group of professionals.

It wasn't any use going on through the night. Fumbling around in the dark would probably only end up with one of them being injured or lost; they would be leaving an easy trail for their pursuers. They both spent the night taking turns trying to sleep and keeping watch, but it was hard to sleep, not knowing if at any moment the men chasing them were sleeping, too, or pushing on through the night.

After a very restless night's sleep, the two of them were both up early and on the way. No fire during the night had meant a cold night's sleep, but being on the move would soon have them warmed up. Dylan was worried about his friend's injured foot. He had noticed late last night he'd started to limp, but he knew that Matt wouldn't say anything. He could only hope they could push through and lose any possible pursuit.

It was late in the afternoon when they finished climbing a high peak that they hadn't been able to go around when Dylan and Matt noticed something they both wished they hadn't seen. About two to three hours behind at most, lower down the slope, they could see four men moving quickly up the mountain trail that the two of them were on.

"Damn. They have been gaining on us, probably started earlier and stopped later." Matt was shaking his head as he spoke, looking through the binoculars. "We have to move, Dylan. I don't think we can outrun them, or lose them. They are sticking to our trail pretty damn well; one of them down there is an experienced tracker," Matt said.

"I know. The only thing we can do is try to find somewhere to take advantage of the weapons we have. We can't go head-to-head with those high-powered rifles; they have a lot more range than us. The only advantage we have is surprise. We'll choose where and when this fight takes place!" Dylan had a determined look on his face as he spoke, but he was worried, and so was Matt. The odds were now definitely not in their favor, and Dylan couldn't see how either of them were going to get out of this alive.

It was an hour later when Matt and Dylan crested another small rise that dropped down into a valley before rising again; it was the first opportunity Dylan could see where they might be able to thin out the men following them.

"I'm going to stop here and wait for them to come up on us, Matt. They can't be more than an hour behind now and we need to slow them down. With your foot the way it is, you need to keep moving and I'll try to catch you, if all goes well," Dylan told his best friend. "And Matt, I don't want any arguments from you either. This is the way it has to be." Dylan patted him on the back, and Matt hugged him back.

"Okay, but just don't go being a hero on me, okay! I want you back, and let's be honest, Brea would give me hell if I go home without you!" Matt was looking as close to upset as Dylan had ever seen him, so he only nodded, gave his friend a pat on the back, and pushed him on his way up the hill.

"Get going, Matt, don't stop or wait for me, okay? If all goes well, I'll catch up to you, and if not, well, just keep moving." Dylan started to move into a more heavily wooded area of the slope where he could see the trail cut through the rocks, but the trees would still give him some cover from those pursuing him.

Matt was a little way up the trail now and wouldn't waste the advantage his friend's sacrifice had given him, no matter how much it hurt him to walk away. Dylan had picked his spot well and laid out his bow and three arrows next to him on the ground within easy reach. He put down three arrows, but at best he would only be able to shoot twice, and if things went really bad, only once. He was hoping to put at least one of the four men down, if he was lucky then maybe two of them. Even two wounded would be better than nothing, as they would hold up the others, if not force them to turn back.

Time seemed to slow down as Dylan waited for the men to come up the trail behind them—it often did for Dylan during stressful times like this—almost like his soul was giving him time to look back on everything he had done or those close to him. He was hoping that he could get this over with sooner rather than later, and not feel as if he was spending an eternity waiting. The adrenaline would be kicking in any second giving Dylan just the boost he needed; maybe it would be enough of an advantage to get him out of this tight spot that he and Matt had put themselves in.

Fifteen minutes had passed before Dylan noticed the bird burst from the bush just down the trail from him; they were even closer than he thought. He took up his bow, nocking an arrow, and took the weight of the string, every muscle in his chest and arms straining as he stretched the bowstring to its maximum.

As he saw the first man clear the rise in the trail, he slowed his breathing down and allowed himself to relax just like his uncle had taught him many years ago. He'd decided to let at least two of the men round the corner before he would take his first shot which would give him much better odds at getting a second shot in. As the second man in the group carefully made his way into view Dylan relaxed his lungs let his breath out and, without even really aiming, let the arrow fly towards its mark. Dylan had learned long ago that you didn't aim so much as just visualize where you wanted the arrow to go, and then, just let your body's muscle memory take care of the rest. Before the first arrow had even found its victim, he had a second arrow drawn and was adjusting his aim onto the man in the front position; the one who had been tracking them so well. As he let the second arrow go, the first arrow took the second man in line clean through the neck, with only the slightest dull thud, as he was lifted up, off his feet, and then slammed off the trail and into the brush.

It was the noise of the first arrow striking that saved the tracker's life. He turned at the last second, and the arrow meant for his heart grazed across his shoulder and deflected off into the brush. The scout had enough instinct to drop and roll away from where he thought the arrow had come from. He also had enough time to warn those coming up behind them, just on the off-chance they had missed their friend being killed in front of them.

Dylan cursed under his breath as he rose and grabbed up the third arrow he still had laying in front of him. He wouldn't get another chance like that, not now that he'd killed one man, but the tracker was only wounded and probably not enough to slow him down or put him out of the chase.

As he started to run up the hill, the rapid crack of an assault rifle on three-round burst could be heard coming from below him. The distinct triple tap cut through the silence of the forest around them, but he couldn't clearly hear where the rounds were impacting.

That was one good thing at least, he thought, as he moved up the hill; they didn't know exactly where he'd taken his shots from so they were shooting wild. They would be that much more careful as they came up after him.

Dylan had to push hard now; those guys down there had more than enough firepower between the three of them to put an end to him and Matt, more than once over. As he ran through the trees, all attempts at stealth abandoned now, rounds were finding their way closer to where he was running. Dylan just hoped the thirty-minute head start he'd given Matt had been enough for his friend to get away, and even better if those three that were left chasing him thought that he'd been acting alone.

The sounds of firing were getting heavier now as Dylan ran. The rounds whipping past his head told him that the three men pursuing him had a fairly good idea of where he was, and where he was going. He risked a quick glance over his shoulder as he ran and saw not too far behind a quick blur as one of the men ducked from out of cover to take several shots at him.

Dylan knew he'd have to make a stand sooner or later, and as he jumped a log, he spun around and pulled another arrow up to his bow. He saw one of the men come into view with his rifle already raised and aimed in his direction. Just as Dylan saw him and knew that he wouldn't be quicker in this battle—the other man had the advantage—a blur came from his right, and he could see the red feathers of an arrow sticking out of the man's chest.

Dylan was staring in the direction the arrow had come from when he saw Matt wave and then start moving up the hill parallel to his position. Dylan started laughing out loud at his crazy bloody friend! He was supposed to be thirty minutes away, safe and sound, but at least now no matter what happened they wouldn't be alone, and now the odds were even.

They both moved closer together as they moved up the hill. They angled their paths so that they would come together somewhere close to the top. Rounds started shredding the leaves above both their heads as Dylan pushed Matt down behind a small mound of dirt, and then fell on top of him. No sooner had they hit the ground than a huge explosion shook the earth directly where they had been, showering them both with large amounts of soil and rocks.

"Hand grenades!" Matt shouted to his friend as he tried wiggling his way down deeper into the ground underneath them.

Dylan was trying to push his way further into cover when he saw Matt lift his head slightly, and something struck him, a bloody red gouge appearing on his best friend's head, as he was whipped sideways, his body falling unnaturally.

"No!" Dylan screamed, as his friend's body lifelessly rolled to one side.

Dylan drew his bow and stood screaming as another explosion knocked him backward, his whole world going black The last thing he saw as he crumpled to the ground was his best friend dead and covered in blood on the ground next to him.

CHAPTER 11

Ricer and his people had been on the move for over three weeks. They were tired and dirty, but apart from that, they were all still in pretty good spirits. Everyone was getting along. Both Brent's and Jess' people were getting along a lot better and had even begun to form a much more effective combat force.

Ricer had been driving them all hard for the past three weeks, trying to push out this patrol as quickly as possible to see if they could find any scattered survivors and then bring them into their growing city at Lake Dakota.

So far they hadn't had a lot of luck—a couple of drifters that they had fed and sent back in the general direction of the Lake—but no large camps or communities that they were looking for. They had been pushing hard most of the day trying to clear a large range of mountains before sunset so they could camp on the other side and have a good easy march. Ricer's forward scouts sent a report back that they had heard gunshots at the front of the patrol, most likely the other side of the ridge.

As the rest of the patrol double-timed it up the

mountain, Ricer started to hear more gunshots and what sounded like quite a gun battle happening just below them.

They all crested the rise and his scouts were carefully, and as quickly as possible, pushing down toward where the gunshots were coming from. Ricer was looking down from the crest with his binoculars trying to work out exactly what the hell was happening below him before he walked into the middle of a firefight. He could make out two men running away from two other men armed with what looked and sounded like high-powered assault rifles. The two younger men were armed with bows. Despite the way they moved through the woods, Ricer didn't think they would make it much further before their luck ran out.

"Brent, Jess! Take half your squads to either flank and push them down the mountain either side. Keep a good distance; we don't know if there are more people out there, okay? Then send the rest of the patrol straight through the center!" Ricer was talking to each of them, but not looking. He was determined not to look away in case he missed something important; he was studying what was happening through his binoculars.

They both knuckled their heads in a quick salute and then split their men and headed off to either flank. There were no screaming or shouting—professionals that they were—they just got it done.

"The rest of you men are with me; we're going straight down the middle. I'm not sure what's going on down there, but those two with the bows are in trouble and the others with the assault rifles are giving them a pasting!" Ricer wasn't messing around, and neither were his people.

They all moved down the hill, double time, moving

from cover to cover, each man taking a firing position covering the man ahead as they leapfrogged forward. Ricer threw himself to the ground as a series of explosions blasted somewhere to the front of where he was leading his men. Ricer looked around until he spotted who he was looking for and threw his rifle up to his shoulder.

"You, put your weapons down!" He shouted at one of the men dressed in camouflage standing in front of him. Two of his men moved up to cover him.

"You are surrounded by an armed patrol of the U.F.P.! Drop your weapons and get down on the ground!" The man hadn't moved, not even an inch.

Ricer didn't hear whatever it was that he said, it sounded like a muttered curse before the guy started to swing his rifle towards him. Ricer pulled the trigger on his own weapon the same instant that the man's chest seemed to explode as over a dozen individual rounds blew the man backward into the brush, his body rolling away down the hill.

The squad with Ricer kept moving down the trail and had the last man pinned down behind a large rock, rounds throwing chunks of stone in all directions as they all pounded his position. When he rose from cover, he started to scream a blood-curdling war cry, firing on them with his rifle on fully automatic.

Somewhere to Ricer's left a single shot took the shooter through the side of the head, the round and what was inside his skull exiting through the much larger hole on the other side of his head; He crumpled lifelessly to the ground.

"Spread out! I want three men to stay with me to check on those two dead guys with the bows. The rest of you spread out and make sure there aren't any more hostiles in the area." Ricer started moving away to where he had last seen those other two guys take cover when someone started shouting to get his attention.

"Sir, sir! These two guys—they're both alive."

CHAPTER 12

Dylan's whole head was screaming at him, as if someone was running a power saw through his face; that's what it felt like anyway as he lay slowly trying to work out if he was alive or dead. Alive, definitely alive, he thought to himself; nothing could hurt this much if he were dead. He was opening his eyes slowly, trying to look around, but it was all blurry and dark. Just this small act felt like torture to him.

He was trying to work out where he was, but it was hard. As far as he could tell, he was lying on a stretcher, but that's not right, he thought, confused. The last thing he remembered was he was trying to burrow into the ground, as the whole world exploded around him. Matt, where was Matt? He was trying to move his head desperately now to look around, but he just couldn't seem to move enough.

"Matt!" He screamed out loud. It wasn't that much of a scream, but it was the best that he could come up with that was anything close to resembling a scream. His damn throat was so dry.

"Matt! Hello? Anyone?" Nothing. Goddamn it.

Now he really wanted to know what the hell was going on, where was his best friend and where exactly was he, dead or alive. If he was dead, it sucked, and it hurt. He must be alive.

"Dylan, welcome back, my name is Ricer, and you're safe here. Just relax and breathe, take it easy, you have been through quite a lot." Ricer placed his hand on Dylan's shoulder reassuringly as he spoke, reaching for a glass of water on the floor next to Dylan, offering it to him

"Where is Matt? Where is my friend? Where am I?" Dylan was trying to be calm, but he couldn't relax until he knew what was going on.

"Your friend is okay. He is asleep next door. He was pretty shaken up from the fight; he has a whole mess of shrapnel wounds and at least two small bullet wounds. One of our medics is with him right now; he's in safe hands. If you look down, you'll notice that you look a lot like Swiss cheese yourself, Dylan. We are from the U.F.P.; we were patrolling in the hopes of bringing new people like yourself and Matt into our community at Lake Dakota. Matt has explained a little about you and him and what was happening with those guys, but apart from that he hasn't said a whole lot of anything. He's been waiting for you to wake up. I'll bring him to see you as soon as possible, okay? But for now, drink some more water and rest, please; you're safe here, so just relax, okay?" Ricer patted his shoulder and slowly stood and walked out.

From what Dylan could now see, he was in a tent of some sort. Suddenly he felt exhausted. He let his head relax, closed his eyes and let himself sink into the mattress. Knowing that Matt was alive was all that he cared about at this point. He drifted off to sleep.

It felt like he had been asleep for a week when he opened his eyes and looked around his makeshift room once again.

"Hello, stranger!" Matt was sitting off to one side beaming at him with that stupid grin again.

"I never thought you would wake up, sleeping beauty! I have a lot to fill you in on, Dylan," Matt spoke softly, not wanting to make too much noise.

"Matt! You don't know how bloody happy I am to see you!" Dylan exclaimed, as both friends quickly embraced.

Matt started to fill his friend in on everything he had learned about the people and the camp, while Dylan had been recovering, also what had happened that he could remember of the fight.

"That guy Ricer seems legit, Dylan, as far as I can tell anyway. His men have nothing but good things to say about him, the squad leaders, and the U.F.P. in general. Their main city or base of operations at Lake Dakota is apparently quite big and they have established a democratic stronghold there. Dylan, these are the guys we were looking for, we found them; Not only that, they saved our lives back there." Matt had been listening and learning to find out whatever he could before he let Ricer know too much about him and Dylan, or their friends and families back at the compound.

"Okay. Well, I trust your judgment on this; let's talk to this Ricer guy and see what he can offer our people and us before we decide if we take them all to our people." Dylan was nervous; this was a big step for the whole compound. He wasn't going to rush into anything just because they seemed okay and had saved their lives.

"Ricer wants to meet with us as soon as you're up for it,

Dylan. We can talk to him then and see what his plans are and what he wants from us. Until you're ready, just relax and try to take it easy. You lost a massive amount of blood. You've been out three days already, buddy." Matt embraced his friend and walked out.

Dylan was tired—even just this small bit of activity had drained him already. Even though he wasn't that hungry, he reached over and started to eat the ration pack meal that had been left for him. He ate it all and drank as much water as he could.

It wasn't long before he was drifting off to sleep. When he woke he'd be in much better shape and ready to speak with Ricer to find out what he had for his family and him.

Dylan and Matt were taken to Ricer's main tent in the camp. He had a meal of rations ready for both of them, as well as chairs set out for them. He also had his two squad leaders with him, Jess and Brent; they were sitting off to one side but still positioned so they could be part of the meeting.

"Dylan, Matt, sit down and have something to eat, please. Matt, you already know Brent and Jess; they are my Squad Leaders. Normally they would be leading their own teams, but we are trying to push out a recon in force to bring in new people. It's lucky for you two that we came along when we did. Otherwise, you would both be fertilizing the forest out there. Those guys you killed, and the ones we killed that were chasing you, were Mercury Tech members." Matt and Dylan both looked at each other the second they heard the name come out of Ricer's mouth. Mercury Tech, or the MTs, as they were known, was the worst of the worst.

They were the first of the private security firms

employed by the government who went rogue. They started the slaughter, and up until communications ceased and the government control broke down completely, were fighting a cruel, bloody civil war, killing everyone they came across—men, women, and children.

The only thing that stopped them from taking complete control was often as not, they were fighting amongst themselves in a never-ending internal power struggle. The last Dylan had heard about the MTs was they were under an instant death sentence, and were to be taken dead or alive, but preferably dead.

"Yeah, that's right, MTs. The big, bad, bogeymen that even the bad guys out there are scared of. Don't get me wrong. I have a bad ass group of people; some of the most decorated and highly-trained operators, but the MTs are monsters. It explains why they didn't throw down when we rolled up on them. We would have killed them afterward anyway, just for past crimes committed, and they knew it. From what Matt tells me, you killed three of them before we got there, and you did it with nothing more than bows. That's pretty damn impressive. You have some bad ass in yourselves, too! It also explains why you two are out here all alone, and even now, you don't seem scared at all, just wary. So, Matt and Dylan, what are you two doing out here miles away from home, and all alone?" Ricer left the question hanging. There were a few awkward minutes of silence as Matt and Dylan looked at each other, trying to gauge how much they should let Ricer and the others know.

"We are here looking for you, Ricer. Well, not you, personally, but the U.F.P. You see, we have family back in a small compound a few weeks' march away, and we decided it was time we became part of the world. We decided the time for hiding away in our compound was over; we want to live, not just be alive. We want to become part of something bigger; we were hoping that the something bigger could be with you." Dylan looked at Ricer as he delivered his small speech.

"Well, it looks as if you found us and we would be happy to have you and your people. That's after we meet them all, of course. I'd like to welcome you personally to the U.F.P., and I'd like to get moving and meet the rest of your families if you two are up for it." Ricer stood and extended his hand for Matt and Dylan to shake.

"Welcome, it's time to be part of something bigger, Dylan. We are rebuilding the country, then the continent, and after that, hell, the whole wide world!"

CHAPTER 13

The last month in the compound had passed pretty slowly for Brea and Seb. The poor weather was definitely not helping the situation one bit. Not knowing if Dylan and Matt were okay was weighing pretty heavily on Brea. It hadn't helped her mood which swung from sad to angry, at the drop of a hat. Seb had been on the receiving end of more than one of his older sister's angry rants. Ten minutes later they would switch to a flood of tears, and finally end in her running away to her room, slamming the door behind her.

It wasn't Seb's fault and she told him so every time. He had reassured her that he understood, but it didn't make her feel any less guilty or make him feel any better about being his sister's punching bag.

Brea knew deep inside her heart that they were both still alive, they just had to be. If they had died, then she would be able to tell. She had a link to them and the link hadn't been broken. The compound was gearing up for winter and had been gathering and preserving food and fuel to store for the coming winter months. The first few winters after the virus had swept through the country had been the hardest the compound had ever faced. There had been several deaths; the weak and the elderly had been the worst affected by the bitter cold.

Every winter they had survived since had taught them something new, which had made them tougher and more prepared for the next winter. The council had set certain people different jobs. It was up to them to not only complete their tasks, but report their results to the council so it would be aware of the progression of their tasks.

Hunters were out every day, as long as there was light, and sometimes even into the darker hours, bringing in as much meat as possible to be stored. All wild fruits and vegetables that had been painstakingly cultivated during the years were harvested, the seeds collected, and foods stored away to last them through the heavy snows when nothing would be grown. Wood had been stored to provide heating and fuel as the small amount of electricity they produced during the shorter, darker days of winter would be greatly reduced. Fresh water tanks had been filled and covered, as much as possible, to prevent them freezing over so they wouldn't have to waste the stored wood heating and melting ice for drinking water.

Everyone had reported at the last council meeting they were ahead of schedule, and if all went well, would probably have a very decent safety buffer of about 20% above what they expected to need for the winter months.

The council had been carefully conducting some inspections all over the compound, going over the whole area inch by inch. They checked the walls, everyone's living quarters, community areas, and store rooms, making sure any damage found was repaired. It was important they made the necessary repairs now, while they still had the chance. Their number one priority was the health and safety of everyone inside the walls; ensuring the walls on the perimeter of the compound were as strong as possible was normally the first and last thing checked.

With Dylan and Matt both away, they were down two of their best hunters, but that hadn't worried the community at all. They had all picked up the extra slack and had achieved an even better than expected result.

Brea knew that this was going to be hard with both Dylan and Matt away, and she didn't expect them back for anywhere up to another four weeks, right before winter totally closed them off. This had been the longest she and Seb had been separated from Dylan since the virus had swept away their parents in its tidal wave of death.

Her moods hadn't helped at all. To top it off, she hadn't been feeling well lately, her appetite going from non-existent to ravenously hungry at the flick of a switch. "Goddamn you, Matt! And damn you, Dylan, as well!" She yelled at the walls, desperately trying not to smash her hands against the hard walls of the compound.

"Are you okay, sis?" Seb had come downstairs to see what the yelling was about and to make sure his sister was okay, which was becoming a full-time job lately, all by itself.

"Yes, as well as I can be. I just wish that I could shake this flu, I never get sick," Brea said.

"Have you heard something, are they back?" Seb asked.

Brea hadn't meant to worry him, and now the questions were flooding out of him faster than she could hope to answer them.

"No, sorry, Seb. I haven't heard anything. I was just yelling out loud, sorry. I'm just frustrated is all. I just wish there was some way that we could talk to them, just to see if they are okay. You know what I mean? I never miss cell phones, until either your brother or Matt is away from home," Brea spoke softly, pulling up a chair and flopping into it, emotionally drained.

"They'll be fine, Brea. I know they will, and so do you. Dylan and Matt are freaking tough asses, okay?" Seb was getting good at this part of it. It was the tears that he hadn't quite learned to deal with; it was just so unnatural to see his sister vulnerable.

"I know, I'm stupid; it's just that I've never been away from either of them longer than a day or two in the last ten years. I never thought it would be this hard on me." Brea was staring off into the distance.

Seb moved over to his older sister and hugged her into him tightly as she sobbed on his shoulders.

"We will be okay. So will they. We just need to make sure we keep thinking positive thoughts. No more tears, okay? If you need anything, remember, just ask," Seb replied.

"You don't understand how much I appreciate everything you have been doing around here, Seb, and around the compound, too. You're finally starting to turn into an adult, thank you," Brea said to Seb, hugging him back tightly.

As she sat hugging Seb, Brea couldn't help but hope that Matt and Dylan would return home soon.

CHAPTER 14

They had been making pretty good time so far. Dylan was surprised with just how hard Ricer had been pushing his people, and how well they were all taking it. There was no grumbling or whining, they just dug a bit deeper and kept on picking up the pace. Up a hill, or across a river, it didn't seem to matter to these guys and girls; they just kept on eating up the miles.

Ricer had been calling Matt and Dylan to eat with him most evenings so they could talk about where he was from, who he worked for, what the city was like, and the things he had done before and after the virus had struck. He had just as many questions for them about the people back at the compound, too. They normally just relaxed, ate, and spoke for a couple of hours every evening. The chats didn't last much longer than that, despite the fact that they were all in good shape; everyone was well and truly exhausted by the end of the day.

They were taking a different route back to the compound. Ricer was using a set of maps he'd dug up from somewhere and was trying to take a path that could lead him past any possible places where people might have taken refuge and set up safe areas or compounds. Dylan and Matt had both already spent many hours studying the maps, and tried to help by marking any spots where they'd seen people, or where they hadn't come across anyone at all.

Both of them had been recovering quite quickly from their wounds, and Ricer hadn't had to slow down for them after the first week. Even Matt's foot had come along nicely with a decent amount of antibiotics and the care of one of the first aid people attached to Ricer's patrol. That hadn't stopped the entire group from calling him Bunny after Dylan had told them the rabbit trap story.

After the first week of taking it easy, they had both been spreading out either side on the flanks or moving forward to help take turns acting as scouts to try and take a little bit of the load off the patrol's men. If they got a little bit of a break, they would all be more rested and capable of moving even quicker.

The season's first snow had started to fall; they had all started to use the tents and ground covers of a night whenever they stopped. It was taking them longer and cutting down on their rest time, but it was a lot better to have decent shelter and somewhere to dry out their clothes and boots, even just a little bit.

The winds which normally blew up at this time of year had already been making their presence felt among the group. Once the patrol moved out of the shelter of the forest, it would make the miles across more open terrain a lot more uncomfortable.

As the second and third weeks moved on without anything significant happening, even Dylan and Matt's luck hunting for fresh meat had started to run out. More and more they all had to rely on their ration packs and dried meat. It was pretty much all they had left.

Everyone was excited and curious about watching and learning whenever Matt and Dylan had their bows out and were practicing. Two or three people had been quietly watching and learning from them whenever they got the chance. It wasn't as if they didn't have bows back at the city, but with the weapons and ammunition they had somehow managed to accumulate over the years, they just didn't have to rely on them as much as people out in the wilds did.

So far they hadn't come across any compounds or groups of people. Ricer was starting to think between the virus and the slaughter, the estimates Max had given him on population were a lot lower than either of them had expected.

They had reached the end of the thick forest early in the morning. The trees had started to give way to larger and larger expanses of cleared areas the wind was howling through, even this early in the day. It was a hard march straight into the wind throughout most of the day. Even the seasoned soldiers and hunters were just about completely drained of energy when Ricer called an early halt to the day after receiving some alarming news.

Ricer motioned one of his runners over towards him, as the rest of the men around him were digging out shallow scrapes in the ground to set up their tents and shelters.

"Yes, sir?" the runner asked him.

"Have Jess and Brent come and see me after they have gotten their teams stood down and their sentry posts set out. Also, find those two Wilders for me, Dylan and Matt; they will be out with the scouts somewhere, I expect. I want them all to come in for a briefing, as quickly as possible." Ricer dismissed the runner with a wave of his hand, turning and rubbing his jaw as he thought. The runner knuckled a brief salute to Ricer and then made his way to the camp to start on his task of rounding up everyone as fast as he could. The longer he took, the less time he'd have to eat and sleep.

Brent and Jess showed up first, within about thirty minutes. Dylan and Matt were almost an hour later, as they had both been a lot further forward from the main body of the patrol. It took them a while to work their way back to the camp.

"What do you think Ricer wants?" Matt asked Dylan as they walked towards his tent.

"I'm not sure, Matt, but it must be something important if he has taken the time to have us called all the way into the main camp," Dylan answered his friend.

"I guess we'll find out, eh," Matt replied as they approached Ricer's command tent and walked in.

"Come in; take a seat if you like. I have some news from one of our scouts out on the eastern flank of the main patrol. Today, the scout spotted smoke and not just a single small campfire either. From his estimates, it's at least three or four different fires, most likely a small settlement. After he had reported this back to me, I sent him and another scout off to get a closer look and check it out. As of when I called you all in, I hadn't heard back from either of them; they have disappeared. So I want everyone around the camp, every soldier, to be extra vigilant tonight. We need to ensure that we set double sentries, and be extra vigilant. Okay?" Ricer told them all.

"What's the plan if we don't hear back from the scouts; have we got anyone out looking for them?" Brent asked.

"Yes. I sent four of my guys to follow their tracks. They

have strict orders not to endanger themselves in any way; they are strictly to observe and report. We need to get intelligence—intelligence we can act on. First thing tomorrow, if we still haven't heard anything, then we are all going to go and find out what's happened," Ricer told them all.

"Are there supposed to be any large settlements in this area?" Matt asked.

"No, of all the areas we had marked down, this one was probably one of the least likely to have any civilians in it. There just aren't a lot of infrastructures reported to have been here before things started to break down," Ricer answered.

"What do you think happened, then?" Dylan asked.

"Best scenario, they're lost. The worst scenario is they have been killed or captured by a large group similar to ours," Ricer replied.

"Sir, no disrespect, but our scouts don't get lost; it just wouldn't happen," Jess replied.

"Jess, I know. Until we find out more information, we need to hope for the best, but assume the worst. We'll know more in the morning. Get your people organized, get some rest, but be ready to go first thing in the morning. You're all dismissed; I'll let you know the minute I find anything out." Ricer waved them out as he finished speaking.

He hated it; the not knowing what was happening was crippling to him. It wouldn't be the first time Ricer had lost people, but he definitely didn't like to make a habit of it. If it ever got easier, he would probably retire on the spot. They all moved off to their men and tents, had something to eat, and got ready to sleep for the night. No matter what happened it would be a long day ahead for all of them.

The next day, well before the sun had begun to rise over the mountains, the camp was up, and they were preparing to move out. They still didn't have a lot of information, but they would be heading in the direction where the scouts had last been reported.

The mood among the men and women was extremely tense. Among such a close group of people, it didn't matter who was in trouble; whenever one of their own was in any sort of trouble, it was like a family member was in trouble. Dylan hadn't seen them pack up their camp and move out this fast the entire time he had been traveling with them.

He was about a week away from his own home and family. He was pretty eager to get back and see they were all okay. The closer the group got to his home, the more anxious he became. So far there hadn't been any signs of this mysterious camp or the campfires which the scouts had been sent to investigate in the first place.

They were still probably an hour's march away, but Dylan thought it was strange he hadn't seen any sign of people at all. Dylan motioned Matt over to him, and they had a quick discussion about it.

"Listen, if there were a large group of people around here, there would be a lot more signs. People leave trails, no matter how much they try not to, especially when you have a compound full, that's why we always limit who can go in and out all the time," Dylan said to Matt.

"I know; I was thinking the same thing, Dylan," Matt answered. "This close to any camp there should be tracks everywhere as people come and go, and even signs from where they had been foraging for supplies."

"Just be bloody careful, Matt, I don't want to have to explain to Brea why I let you get killed so close to home.

Not after everything that we have been through," Dylan said. Matt just laughed.

"Not likely, buddy!" Matt punched his friend on the shoulder and jogged back to join the troops he'd been working with. Typical Matt, Dylan thought, as he chuckled to himself. He'll get me bloody skinned alive one day.

The order came down the line for them to hold up and take a five-minute break while the scouts pushed forward to see what was in front of them. It wouldn't do anyone any good if they all walked into an ambush.

Dylan and Matt moved up to get into a position to head out with the scouts. They wanted to be close to the front so they could get a look for themselves at what was going on. If they were walking into something, they wanted to have all the information first-hand, not being passed down the line.

The scouts at first hadn't been overly enthusiastic about either Matt or Dylan; who could blame them? Trained soldiers spent their entire lives working together; having two complete strangers thrust upon them went against all their instincts. It didn't take long for them to get over it after Dylan and Matt had proved what they were capable of. They had been welcomed like long-lost family members.

Even for professional soldiers, the mood up front was pretty tense. All the scouts had wanted to go out last night to see what could have happened to their friends, but Ricer hadn't allowed it. He told them all, with good reason, that it was too dangerous. He couldn't afford to lose any more of the team.

The forward scouts had reported back to the remainder of the scouts they had found what appeared to be a small group of buildings and were holding position to await backup and further orders.

When Dylan and Matt moved up to them, the scouts were all sitting approximately a quarter of a mile from a small camp. They reported there weren't any visible signs of either smoke or people. The scouts were all dropping their packs and stripping down their gear so they could move as quickly as possible. If they had to fight, they wanted to be as light as possible to allow for faster reaction times and movement.

It was almost twenty minutes later when Ricer and the main group moved up into position and the scouts could give a full report of what they had observed so far. Ricer stood watching the buildings through his binoculars while the scouts told him everything they had learned.

"Okay, I want the scouts to move in from all sides simultaneously. They will be the lead on this approach, the rest of the patrol is to maintain a safe distance, but be ready to roll upon the objective should contact be initiated. Make sure you maintain constant radio updates with each other. I want to know what's going on at all times. At the first sign of trouble, call it over the net and we will push in both patrols." Ricer was sketching an outline of the camp from what the scouts had reported as he spoke to them all.

"Be careful, everyone. I don't know what's happened with two of our people and I can't afford to lose anymore. Okay, you know what to do, let's get it done." There were no more questions; everyone was clear on what they needed to do. They all saluted and moved off to inform their teams and get into their jumping-off positions.

Dylan and Matt had been told they could join up with the group going to the rear of the camp. They started to drop their gear so they would be able to move quickly and quietly. This was no time to be carrying full packs of gear that could get in the way; there would be plenty of time to gather their stuff later.

They both had their bows and pistols, but neither had bothered with the assault rifles they had been offered. They signaled over the radio they were ready and then heard back from each of the other groups as they all signaled back they too were ready to move in.

The back of the camp had a large wooden wall approximately fifteen feet high that looked like a rush job; it looked like it wouldn't stop anyone determined from getting in, only curious people. From what Dylan could guess from this distance, it had only been there around six months. That would explain why there wasn't a lot of signs about the camp, Dylan thought; it hadn't been around long enough to create much of a disturbance in the area outside of the wall.

They all moved into position and threw several sets of grappling hooks up and over the wall. They could have blown the wall down without a lot of trouble, but it would have given away their advantage of surprise.

The first two guys who made it to the top of the wall then helped the next two up and so on, until the forward team was all inside the camp walls. The scouts all broke into pairs; this way they would have some support if anything happened while they were searching the camp.

So far the reports coming in over the net were all similar: no resistance and no one sighted yet either. It looked like the camp was empty at this point. If no one had spotted that smoke the day before, they would have assumed it had been empty for weeks. If they didn't know better, it looked like the camp had been built and deserted a long time ago, but they did know better.

Suddenly, a panicked voice broke in over the radio net, saying they had located the scouts towards the front section of the camp; they sounded frightened and also worried. It took a lot to create any fear in men such as these.

"Are they alive?" Ricer asked, breaking in over the radio, a sense of urgency and determination in his voice.

"No, sir. Sir, someone killed them. It's not pretty, sir, you'd better come and check this out for yourself, they..." The Scout leader in charge of the patrol who had been tasked with going to clear the front section of the camp near the gates didn't get an opportunity to finish what he was about to say before Ricer cut him off.

"What's happened?" Ricer asked urgently.

"Sir, with all due respect, I think that it's better if you come and see this for yourself. I don't want to talk about it over the open radio," the patrol leader replied, his voice getting faint, almost nervous.

"Okay, I'll be there myself in ten minutes. Keep it closed off; make sure no one else goes in until I check it out. Over," Ricer replied, shutting off the radio and moving in toward the camp.

Dylan called Matt over to him as they were moving through the camp.

"Did you hear that?" Dylan asked quietly.

"Yeah buddy, that sounds like all kinds of messed up. Something bad must have happened for these guys to sound so worried. Keep your eyes on a swivel, Dylan," Matt replied as they started to move away.

They kept moving through the camp, more slowly than before, neither of them taking any chances. They didn't know what had happened yet, but whatever it was, it didn't sound good. They took their time, checking out all the different small buildings and structures, making sure there wasn't anyone lurking around.

By now they had finished the middle section of the camp and hadn't discovered anything useful, and now were at the front section of the camp where most of the team seemed to be gathered. When they approached the last two buildings near the front section of the camp, they noticed there was a large group of scouts who had gathered around one building in particular.

Suddenly the door burst open, and a scout walked out and threw up all over the muddy ground, walking several more feet, then doubling up and retching again.

"That doesn't look good at all, Dylan," Matt said as he shook his head.

Dylan moved up to the building which the scout had walked out from, but as he got close to the door of the building, one of the other scouts put his arm out and blocked the door.

"You don't want to go in there. It isn't good; no one needs to see that." He shook his head and even the tough-looking veteran had a shaken and pale expression on his face.

Just then Ricer walked out through the door, his face pale, and he looked visibly shaken. Dylan had never seen someone burning with such a fury, the way Ricer looked as his expression changed.

"What happened, Ricer?" Dylan asked him.

"They goddamn tortured them! Animals! I'll kill them all, and they will get back everything that they dished out, times ten." Ricer turned and smashed his fist into the wall next to them both, and didn't even notice the blood running from his knuckles. He pulled his fist back again, and Dylan grabbed his arm and spun him away from the wall.

"Don't! You are the one person who holds this entire group together. They need to see someone they want to be, not someone they are. Wait, for now, let it out when you're alone," Dylan said.

"You're right. Goddamn it, you're right. Thanks," Ricer nodded and moved over to his men guarding the door.

"Clean up that mess in there, clean up our boys. I don't want anyone else to have to see them like that. The rest of you spread out, find out what the hell has been going on here. I want to know who they were, where they went, and when they left. Do it now! Make sure that you do it right. They killed our brothers and we aren't going to stop until we make them pay for it!" Ricer screamed the last bit. A loud chorus of 'yes sirs' went out around the group. They started to divide up the camp into sections so they wouldn't miss anything.

Dylan and Matt moved off together and started to search through the camp as methodically as they could. They had already looked through a large section of it, but a second look wouldn't hurt, it might just reveal the clue that unlocked the puzzle of what had happened.

It wasn't long before Dylan thought he had seen enough to work out what had happened, and he went off in search of Ricer to report what he had discovered. He found Ricer still close to the building where the two bodies had been found. They had been taken out of the building, and now they lay with blankets respectfully covering them.

"What have you found, Dylan, anything?" Ricer asked

Dylan as he walked up towards the group of people standing around the covered bodies.

"Hey, from the tracks and the buildings, I guess there were approximately ten to fifteen of them all totaled. At a guess, I think they left over a week ago. It could be slightly less or more, it's hard to be sure, all the tracks are getting kind of messed up. I think they could have left a couple of their people behind as a rear-guard; they're probably the ones who caught our guys. I don't have a clue who they are. There are a lot of old shell casings around the place and they left a lot of stuff that I wouldn't have. I mean, I don't leave anything, but maybe they were limited by what they could carry, or they were in a hurry." Dylan was starting to get a really bad feeling in his stomach about where these people may have gone. There weren't a lot of places around here worth visiting.

"You think that our guys could have told them about where we were all heading, Ricer?" Dylan motioned with his head at the two bodies lying by their feet.

"Yes, I do. They tortured them too much for them not to. No one could stand up to being skinned alive. Not me, not you, and not Matt, none of us could have," Ricer looked away as he spoke.

"We all need to be out of here as soon as possible, Dylan. I want to get to your people before these animals do. I want you and Matt to take half my scouts and pack light. Get back to your family and I'll follow behind as quickly as I can with the rest of the patrols. Just leave us a trail to follow and we will be right behind you. Okay?" Ricer was staring at him now; he already knew the answer.

"Yep, we will be gone within the hour. Just follow us as best as you can, but I'm telling you now, I won't be messing around. They hurt either my new family or my old family; they'll wish all I was doing was skinning them alive." Dylan had already turned and started to walk towards where he'd last seen Matt speaking to a few of the scouts.

"Good luck, Dylan!" Ricer yelled at his back.

CHAPTER 15

B rea was scared. It was probably the most frightened that she had ever been in the last ten years. All she wanted was Dylan and Matt back; they would know what to do; they always knew what to do. It wasn't until all of this began that she realized how much they all depended on Matt and Dylan.

They had lost four people in the last 48 hours; three more were in a really bad way in the first-aid room. Things had changed three days ago when one of the men on watch up on the wall had called out that he had seen people moving around in the forest opposite the wall.

For the first day, not much had happened, more people had been seen moving around at the edge of the forest, but none had tried to approach the camp. What they hadn't realized, even then, was that the people they all saw had wanted to be seen. The rest of the men had probably been scouting out their defenses and checking for any weak spots. They doubled all the guards on the wall and were extra vigilant about any noises which they heard in the night. Brea was sure that no one in the compound had really slept.

The next day at first light three heavily-armed men in camouflage uniforms had approached the main gates of the compound and asked to speak with whoever was in charge. Anthony had volunteered to go out and talk to them and try to find out who they were and what it was they wanted. No one could hear the conversation, or exactly what had been said, but suddenly the biggest of the three men pulled out a large pistol and shot him in the head. No shouting, no running, he just pulled out his pistol, and, right there in front of them, shot Anthony in the head. Anthony's body was blown off its feet by the force of the impact, the body making a dull thud as it landed on the forest floor at their feet.

They all looked on in shock as the man had walked up close to the walls of the compound.

"You have until noon to abandon the camp and let my men and me in! If you let us in, there doesn't have to be any more bloodshed. No one else has to die! If you don't let us in, we'll come back and let ourselves in, and believe me; you won't enjoy it!" The large stranger shouted, before turning to his companions and laughing. The three men moved back into the woods and two men from the compound quickly went out through the small door to recover Anthony's body.

Brea had called all the remaining compound leaders in for an emergency meeting to try and decide what it was they were going to do.

At the beginning of the meeting, over half of the committee members wanted to rush out of the compound and try to attack the strangers.

"Listen, I know you're all upset, but we have to be smart now! We don't know who these men are, and most importantly, we don't know how many of them there are. We need to wait as long as we can for Dylan and Matt to come back." Brea spoke much more assuredly than she felt inside.

"We don't even know if Matt and Dylan will be back in time, we have to do something!" someone shouted from the back of the room.

"I know what they would have wanted, though, and that would be to play it smart! We have been building this compound for years; we can fight from a position of strength. We need to play it smart." Brea was pleading now; a mad rush into the unknown would leave the rest of the compound too weak to defend them.

The meeting broke down into quiet conversations, but the majority of them decided to try and wait it out. Now they had to get everyone organized; there wasn't any time to waste.

The compound had managed to gather quite a few weapons over the years. They were mostly for defense and wouldn't last long in an assault against well-armed and highly-trained men. Some of the people wanted to try to make an escape before it was too late, but most of them were ready to defend themselves as long as possible. Brea agreed with them; she was hoping that Matt and Dylan would be back in time with help before it was too late.

They decided to stay and fight it out. The hope was by putting up a strong defense, they would make it too costly for the men outside the walls. The rest of that day was spent in strengthening any weak spots on the wall with what they could pull off the buildings and service the weapons they had, ready for the defense of their homes.

It was later that afternoon well after the deadline had passed, but nothing had happened. A few of the people began to suggest that maybe, just maybe, the strangers had moved on to easier pickings.

When the first shot had rung out late in the evening, breaking the silence, no one knew exactly where it had come from. It wasn't long before they found the deadly results. One of the men standing guard at the main gate lay dead. There was a small neat hole in the front of his head, but the back of his head was a bloody, pulpy mess where the high-powered round had exited. Everyone was trying to stay as low as possible after that. They also tried to keep in the cover of the high walls as much as they could, while still trying to keep watch.

An hour later there were two more shots, breaking the terrible silence once again. Two more bodies were found dead on the walls, two more lookouts dead with accurate shots to the head. No one wanted to do watches on the wall anymore, three dead in an afternoon, and Brea couldn't blame them at all. It was hard enough knowing that there were armed men outside the walls, but even harder knowing three good people had already lost their lives on the wall that day.

The rest of the day went by with no more deaths, just ominous silence.

Early the next morning, one of the men's wives who was bringing water and food to the people on guard had been shot in the head. The man could be heard screaming from the walls as his friends tried to hold him back.

Three more people were seriously wounded late in the

afternoon after they had been shot through the walls when they thought they were safe in its cover. Brea and the rest of the council had decided to pull as many people as possible off the walls so they wouldn't be overly exposed to any more of the deadly sniper fire. It just wasn't safe for more than the absolute barest of a presence up there.

Brea wasn't sure if she could do this much longer. All of the tension was starting to fray her nerves really. Seb had started to worry about her; he wasn't sure that she was up to this kind of anxiety. She had started to put on weight as well, even though he hardly saw her eat lately.

As the sun set on another day, Brea did something that she couldn't remember doing in a very long time. She prayed, as hard as she could pray, for Matt and her brother to get back in time to save them all.

CHAPTER 16

Dylan and Matt were exhausted. Dylan couldn't remember ever being this tired and sore before in his entire life, and life had been far from easy. They had hardly slept, and like the rest of the men with them, they were all just running on auto pilot now.

Originally, they had been following the trail of the two men who had killed their friends, but now they were following the trail of the main group. The two men must have caught up with their friends. They had been heading in a steady direction, but once all the men had joined up, the direction had suddenly veered off.

They had all been running at this fast pace for a solid four days now. From what Dylan could tell, they were only three or four days behind the main group. The only problem was Dylan wasn't sure if they could keep up this pace much longer.

From what he and Matt had worked out, they were only two or three days from the compound, which meant that the people they were chasing were most likely already there. The strain must have been showing on his face as he ran because Matt looked over at him then motioned for the men strung out down the trail to stop and rest.

"Dylan, I'm saying this from the very bottom of my heart, buddy, you look like a bucket of warm crap!" Matt laughed as he said it, and then threw his friend a bottle of water. Matt looked at his friend and they both burst out laughing. The rest of the scouts were making signs to each other about crazy Wilders, but both Matt and Dylan had well and truly earned their respect on this march.

"Jackass!" Dylan replied.

"Guys, we are at most two or three days from the compound if we can maintain a decent pace. The people we are chasing are probably already there. By the time we arrive, they would have been there almost three or four days, and after seeing what they did to our men, I don't think they will be messing around," Dylan said to all of the scouts gathered around him in the forest.

"Dylan, we will be useless to them if we run ourselves to death before we even get there," Matt said to his friend. He wanted to get back as much as Dylan, but he was trying to get them there alive, not exhausted.

"I know; I just need to get home, Matt. If something bad has happened, I'll never forgive myself." Dylan shook his head as he spoke and looked off into the distance. It was his responsibility; they were all that he had left in this world apart from his friend.

"Okay, buddy, I understand," Matt replied, and he really did. They both had people they loved back at the compound, people they cared for dearly.

The next day was much like the first ones, but it was just getting much harder now. A couple of the scouts had dropped off the main group; Dylan had told them to catch up as best they could. Every time the group stopped, it was just a little bit harder to force them to get up and start moving again. There wasn't time to rest and wait for the stragglers to catch up; they would have to do the best they could while the rest kept pushing on. Another cold night without any fires or shelters meant they all struggled to sleep, even though most of the group was close to exhaustion.

Matt and Dylan had them up and moving early. Now they were in familiar territory, they were both pushing them all just a little bit harder, if that was even possible. It was midafternoon when Dylan suddenly called them all to a halt, just on the other side of a large clearing. They had lost about three scouts altogether now, and the rest of them, Dylan and Matt included, were close to the point of collapse.

"What's up?" Matt asked as he quietly threw himself down into the soft ground beside Dylan.

"I smelled something—something I haven't smelled in days—smoke. We haven't been lighting any fires, but someone has, and it was very recently. I want to scout around this clearing and check to make sure there aren't any surprises waiting for us. Stay here and gather in the men while I go and check it out," Dylan replied, before darting off into the trees.

Matt just nodded and watched as his friend moved off into the trees. He would be okay; he always was. Matt started to get his gear ready just in case he had to move out quickly to help him.

Dylan was moving a lot slower now through the trees. Every step he took he checked to see where he placed his feet before putting his full weight down. He didn't want a dry branch to crack underneath his feet and let anyone lurking around know he was there.

Almost twenty-five minutes had gone by when his stomach started to feel like he had butterflies in it. Something was wrong; the forest was just too quiet. What people often don't realize is a forest is a noisy place; it was never completely silent.

It wasn't just him being crazy either; he was sure of it. As a seasoned hunter Dylan's senses were going crazy right now—and when his senses told him something—he had learned over the years to pay attention to them.

When he moved further into the forest, he started to understand why. There were two men sitting around what was left of a small fire, probably where they had cooked their last meal only a few hours earlier. Dylan started to notice his first signs on the ground now; these were the two men who had stayed behind at the camp. It looked as if they had set an ambush along the main group's back trail for anyone who was just crazy or dumb enough to rush right into it. He would recognize those two sets of boot prints anywhere.

He'd seen enough now and decided to move back to his group of scouts and bring them up to date with what he'd seen and tell them what he had decided to do.

"There are two of them sitting in a good ambush position about ten minutes up the trail. We could go around them, but if the others come up this trail, they could walk right into them. Or they could get in behind us, and then come upon our rear. Another thing, it's the two from the camp," Dylan said to Matt and the rest of the scouts with them.

"We are not leaving them two; they're not wasting any

more oxygen! Not after what that scum did," said one of the bearded scouts. The rest of the men nodded in agreement.

"I agree. I don't want to leave them either, and after what those two did, I don't think they deserve to see another sunrise. We need to take them out quietly, though. We're only a few hours away from my home, and I don't want any of their friends to know how close we are behind them. Matt and I will take them out with our bows, but I want the rest of you close by in case anything goes wrong. If something happens, we will need to take them out quickly. Okay?" Dylan asked them all. They all nodded in agreement. He quickly filled them all in on where the two men were sitting and what his plan was.

The group all moved off through the forest following Dylan as he carefully retraced his steps to where he'd seen the two men hiding along the trail. Matt and Dylan moved along the path that Dylan had taken earlier, and it wasn't long before Matt was seeing exactly what Dylan had explained to all of them back at the clearing.

The two men hadn't moved much from where they had been sitting; they were both paying attention to anything that was coming up the trail. Dylan assumed they thought they were placed well enough that no one would be able to get in behind them.

"You take the one on the left, Matt; I'll take the guy on the right. Quietly as possible, buddy. Okay?" Dylan told his friend.

Matt nodded to Dylan. There wasn't any need for more words. They both drew two arrows, one they stuck in the ground, and one they notched on their bows. They both took up the slack on the bows and took careful aim, moving to a comfortable crouching position ready to fire.

"Three, two, one, fire!" Dylan whispered to Matt and let his arrow fly towards the man sitting on the right. His arrow flew true to aim and took the man squarely in the middle of his neck. Matt's arrow seemed to hit a small branch, but it was enough to deflect it slightly, taking his intended target in the shoulder close to his neck. As Matt quickly reached for his second arrow, Dylan snatched his up from the ground, stood up, and took aim on the now fleeing man. He let loose and this time, the arrow flew straight and true. It hit the running man cleanly in the back of the neck and exited through the front. The man seemed to trip, fall, and then hit the ground hard. It was only a couple of minutes before the rest of the scouts joined Dylan and Matt. One of them moved to each man and made sure that he was dead.

"Take five minutes, guys. Grab a drink, do something with those two, and then we'll move on. We're getting close to the compound now." Dylan told the scouts then moved off down the trail a bit just to make sure there weren't any more surprises waiting for them.

Matt was watching a couple of the other scouts drag the two men towards the nearest tree and grab some rope that they had found in one of the dead men's packs. It was only a minute before the men were strung up upside down from the tree by their feet. It was a very clear sign for anyone that came to investigate, or to let the rest of the group know they had been there and dealt with the scum.

"Okay, everyone, the compound isn't far now. It's only a few hours at a quick run, but we need to approach with caution. The rest of the group won't be as slack as those two. We need to maintain the element of surprise because we're outnumbered until the rest of the squad catches..." A sound interrupted Dylan mid-sentence, and they all looked off into the distance.

"High-powered rifle," one of the scouts said. Matt and Dylan glanced at each other and stood up quickly.

"We are moving, right now! I'll take the lead with Matt; we aren't stopping until we reach my home!" All of the scouts gathered around Dylan nodded.

They all started to drop as much gear as they could. All they would need was their weapons and ammunition; anything else they could get from the compound. If they were too late to help the people in the compound, then they wouldn't need any of the other gear anyway. Matt and Dylan ran off down the trail as quickly as they could, faster than they had been running the last few days, drawing on the final reserves of strength their bodies possessed.

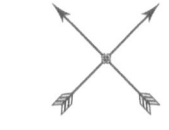

CHAPTER 17

B rea and the rest of the people left in the compound were slowly starting to think that maybe help wasn't coming. Even if it did, it might not make it in time to save them.

They hadn't lost any more people, but as the sun slowly dropped below the mountains, they knew that those people were still out there. It didn't fool any of them for a minute that nothing had happened. Those people were still out there surrounding the camp; they wouldn't be leaving until they had gotten what it was they had come for. Brea had packed as much as she could into two packs in case she and Seb had to get out of the compound quickly, but this was her home, and the people in the compound with her had become her family.

Except for a couple of men who were standing watches as close to the gate and walls as they could get, everyone else in the compound was doing what Brea had just finished doing—packing what they could carry in case the compound was overrun and they had to get out quick.

Brea was armed with a pistol; even Seb was carrying a

handgun along with one of Dylan's old bows. Dylan and Matt had trained them on how to load, shoot, and maintain the pistols, and Brea knew if it came to her or Seb, she would pull the trigger without any hesitation.

Brea sat down in the chair closest to the door. Earlier she and Seb had barricaded the back door and windows as best they could. It would be a long night without any sleep for her. No matter what the long, cold night or the next day brought, she wouldn't go quietly or without a fight.

By now Brea realized she didn't just have the flu either; she was carrying Matt's baby.

CHAPTER 18

Dylan and Matt almost ran straight over the top of the first sentry. He had been that well concealed. He was alongside the trail leading to the rear of their compound.

It was lucky for both of them that he had been asleep. Otherwise, their rescue mission could have been over before it even began. Matt had taken care of the sleeping sentry, quietly slitting his throat in his sleep and then covering him with some branches.

From the tracks they had managed to see before the sun had set completely, there were approximately ten to fifteen men among the larger group. So far, between the two of them they had killed three of them; that still left quite a few men to take care of. they would have to be as careful as possible. If these men were as poorly disciplined as the last sentry, it wouldn't be a bad thing, Dylan thought, but odds were they just got lucky with the last sentry sleeping at his post.

"It won't be long until this guy's friends come to check on him as well as all the other sentries. We have to do whatever we are planning on doing, and do it quickly," Dylan told Matt quietly.

"I want to get inside the compound and check on Brea and Seb, Dylan. We have to make sure that they're okay first. Then we can decide what to do about this lot. Maybe, just maybe, we could stall them until the rest of our guys catch up?" Matt said to his friend.

"I want to check on them, too, Matt, believe me, but once we're in, they aren't going to let us back out again. Getting in will be hard, but getting out could be impossible, no matter how good we are. I want to take out at least another two sentries and then go into the camp. We will wait until the rest of the scouts catch us up before we decide on what we are going to do. They shouldn't be more than thirty minutes behind; then we can come up with a stronger plan. Okay?" Dylan was checking his arrows and making sure everything was firmly attached so that it wouldn't rattle as he spoke to his friend.

It was only fifteen minutes before the rest of the scouts seemed to appear like ghosts out of the forest. Silently they emerged from the dark trees with quick whispers of "a friend, friend," to let Dylan and Matt know who it was sneaking around them.

While Dylan and Matt filled the rest of the scouts in on what they had come up with, and what they were planning, they also sketched a rough map of the compound. On the sketch, they outlined all the buildings, the wall, and the place where Dylan planned to enter through his Narnia gate as Matt liked to call it.

Two of the scouts went with Matt off to the right, while two more went with Dylan to the left. They were hoping to find at least two more of the sentries and take care of them before they made a move into the main compound which would help to even up the odds slightly, still terrible, but what other choice did they have?

It was a little over twenty minutes later when the two groups met back up.

"We found another guy out the back. We took care of him; he won't be waking up anytime soon," Matt told Dylan quietly.

Dylan's group hadn't been as lucky, they had looked for where they thought a sentry would be, but, either he had moved or had been too well hidden for them to find in the dark.

"Let's head into the compound. Once we're inside, I want you guys to wait with Matt while I check on what's happening. We need to make sure they haven't already made it inside and also let everyone know we're here. Once I know what's going on, I'll come back for you with some of our people. We will get you inside the compound, fed, and settled in somewhere. I don't want you guys wandering around in the dark either, just in case someone gets nervous and puts a bullet in you. We have worked too damn hard to get here to have something stupid like that happen now." They all laughed nervously at Dylan's joke, but the truth was it was just as likely they could be shot by one of their friends in the dark, as it was they would be shot by one of the enemies.

Dylan and Matt led the small group towards Dylan's secret entrance into the compound, the Narnia gate, as they were all calling it now. It was only a couple of hours now until the sun would start to shower the countryside with dawn's early light, so they needed to be inside the compound well before that happened.

They all made it to the wall without running into any more of the sentries that were scattered around the perimeter of the compound. It was only another minute or so before they were inside the walls, and waiting quietly crouched in the shadows. One of the scouts moved back to where they had come in and rigged a hand grenade onto the wall. Even though they had tried to cover their tracks, it wouldn't do to lead the bandits straight to where they had gotten in. Just in case they managed to follow their tracks, the grenade would act as an early-warning device. It would also kill whoever wasn't careful enough to check before they stuck their head into the hole.

"Right, wait here with Matt and I'll be back as soon as I can to get you guys. Don't go wandering around. Our guys are all going to be pretty nervous; we don't want any accidents." Dylan patted Matt on the back, and they all nodded to show they understood what he had said.

Each of the scouts covered a different part of their area providing the group with 360-degree arcs of fire, just in case anything happened. It didn't pay to relax, especially when you thought you were safe.

Dylan made his way carefully through the compound. Threading his way around the familiar buildings, it wasn't long before he was standing at the back door to his building. He reached out and carefully tried the back door. It wouldn't budge. He assumed that Brea had barricaded in Seb and herself.

Dylan moved carefully around to the front door being just as quiet as he possibly could and sticking to the shadows. It wouldn't be cool getting shot trying to get into his own building—especially by his own family—not after everything he and Matt had been through so far.

The first thing he did while standing at the front door was try the door to see if it was locked; weird, it wasn't. He hoped that nothing had happened and slowly started to push open the door, keeping low and in the shadows of the front porch.

All of a sudden an explosive sound tore through the silence of the night and a large hole just above Dylan's head appeared in his front door. Seconds later three more equally as loud shots rang out and three more holes appeared in the door. Dylan dove to one side before whoever was sitting inside decided to shift their aim, and he ended up looking like the door, full of holes.

"God damn it! Stop firing! It's me, Dylan!" he shouted as he rolled away from the line of fire. Well, there goes the element of surprise, Dylan thought, as he dragged himself away from the dirt.

"Dylan? Is it really you?" Brea said with a shriek as she burst out of the front door, the smoking pistol still gripped in her hand.

"Yeah, lucky you didn't kill me, sis!" Dylan said from the bushes near the door, standing up and brushing as much dirt off him as he could.

"Oh my god, Dylan, I'm sorry, I thought you were one of them! Thank god, you're back! Wait...

Where's Matt? Dylan, where the hell is Matt?!" Brea shouted, starting to panic as she realized that Matt wasn't with her brother. They were always together.

"Brea, calm down, he's okay! He's waiting for me to come and get him. He's just on the other side of the compound. We were hoping to sneak in, but that didn't work out exactly to plan," Dylan said with a small laugh.

"Get a light going and I'll go and get Matt and the

others. Can you put on some hot food, please? We haven't eaten properly for almost a week," Dylan asked.

Brea hugged her brother and helped him up. Dylan limped off to get Matt and the others.

Lights were coming on all over the compound. She looked around and thought most of the compound must be awake by now if they had even been asleep in the first place; the gunshots taking care of those who had managed to get a few minutes' rest.

Brea moved inside and started to heat up some food on the stove so they would have something hot to eat and some drinks waiting when they got back. Brea was happier than she had been in weeks, her brother was back, Matt was back with him, and now they had a fighting chance to survive this. She allowed herself a small tear, something she had been holding in for weeks; her family might just make it yet!

"Brea, what's going on?" Seb asked from the other end of the building, rubbing his eyes as he walked out of his room where he had been sleeping.

"Matt and Dylan are back, Seb! They have some people with them to help," Brea told her little brother. Seb ran up and jumped on his sister and started to hug her as tightly as he could. He didn't say anything about the tears streaming down her face; he didn't want to embarrass her, but he couldn't help but think to himself he couldn't remember the last time he'd seen her cry.

CHAPTER 19

Ricer was getting pissed. They had been trying to push, but he felt like they were falling behind his scouts, Dylan and Matt.

"How far ahead do you think they are?" Ricer asked one of his scouts who were leading the patrol.

"Best guess, a day and a half, sir, maybe less," the scout replied. Following the others' tracks was making their job easier, but it was still hard for them to keep up with such a fast pace. They didn't have to worry about being ambushed or traps, but they still had to be vigilant.

"Those two bodies we found this afternoon, the ones hanging upside down, were they the same two who tortured my men?" Ricer asked, rubbing his head. He seemed to rub his head whenever he got stressed; he would rub a hole in it at this rate.

"Yep, the boots matched the earlier tracks. I would guess that our boys caught up with them yesterday."

"Okay, good. They deserved a lot worse. I want to push the group now, we could be in the compound within 48 hours, but I want to get there as soon as possible. Early rise tomorrow and fast pace, spread the word. Jess, Brent, let your people know. Get a good night's rest everyone!" Ricer finished speaking, dismissing them with a wave.

As they all walked out of Ricer's tent, Jess and Brent stopped for a moment to speak to each other.

"Fast pace, huh?" Jess asked.

"I know, right? Like we've been out on a summer stroll! Ha, fast pace indeed!" Brent replied as he walked off into the darkness to let his people know of the plan.

CHAPTER 20

Dylan, Matt, and the four scouts quietly moved through the compound. They looked to make sure no one had tried to get into the wall and listened to the people's versions of what had happened.

All possible information was needed if the men had any hope of preventing a disaster. They didn't have to beat the men outside the walls., They had to hold them off until Ricer and the rest of the patrol had time to arrive.

By this time, the people outside the compound would have found their dead men, and know that someone had managed to infiltrate the camp. If they suspected Ricer's group was close, they would need to get inside the compound quickly.

"They know we are here now. They know Ricer and the rest of the patrol will soon arrive. So they need to act, and act quickly," Dylan spoke to the other scouts and some of the compound's leaders inside the small room.

"Maybe they'll leave?" one of the compound's defenders asked.

"Nah, they can't afford to run," the large scout to Dylan's right replied.

"He's right. If they run, they'll have Ricer and the rest of the patrol chasing them and no decent defensible position. What they need is a base, this base," Matt replied as he paced across the room.

"Yep, they will badly want to be in here. They haven't got any time to waste; we need to be ready today. I think they will make a rush at this place, and damn their casualties," Dylan quietly said to the group. He didn't want to make it sound so bad, but sugarcoating their situation wasn't possible.

"The first thing I want to do is try and handle this sniper shooting our people. Ben, Sam? Do you think if I got you one of our scoped hunting rifles you could get setup on top of the water tower and try to take them out?" Dylan asked two of the scouts whom he knew were good shots.

"Sure, not a problem. A hunting rifle isn't a sniper rifle, but we can make do. Do you have a decent pair of binoculars, too?" Sam asked.

"Here, take mine," Matt said handing over his binoculars to the pair.

"Thanks, man. If you guys don't mind, we're going to climb the tower and get ready before the sun rises. If we wait longer, we won't stand a chance," Ben quietly spoke as Sam and he gathered their gear and walked out of the room.

Dylan hadn't faced this sort of attack before. The largest group he had ever had to defend against was only two or three people, nothing like this; not against a group of over a dozen trained men who were determined to wipe them off the face of the earth.

He needed time to think, but there wasn't any time left.

Dylan was supposed to be the leader, and leaders had to make hard decisions; but how do you order ordinary men and women to positions in which they could be killed? He had no more time left to think about it; now there was only time left to act if they wanted to get out of this alive.

"Matt, get everyone organized. We need to man up on the wall as soon as possible. If I'm right, they will try and overwhelm us, use their superior firepower to try and rush our positions, and get through the walls before we can focus any defense." Dylan was trying to get into their heads, imagine what he would do in their situation.

"No worries, Dylan; I'll do it now." Matt motioned to the rest of the scouts, and they quickly filed out of the room.

"Dylan, can I help?" Seb asked, his bow clasped in his hand, a pistol in a holster on his belt. Dylan's first instinct was to protect his family, but what right did he have to place the rest of the compound in danger while his family was kept safe out of the fight. Besides, Seb could shoot, and they needed everyone now.

"Seb, listen," Dylan began.

"I know, Dylan, but you know that I can shoot. I want to help!" Seb seemed to have grown up in the short time since Dylan and Matt had left the compound only a month or so ago.

"Okay, I need you, Seb, but for the love of God, if you get hurt, I'll kill you myself! That is if Brea doesn't get to us first!" Dylan patted his younger brother on the back; the boy had become a man.

"I'm going to be moving around the compound walls, wherever there looks to be any sort of action. I want you to stick to me like glue; I want you so close that by the end of the day my shadow is jealous, Seb. When I say do something or go somewhere, I'll need you to be halfway there already. You understand what I'm saying, Seb?" Dylan asked, looking his brother in the eye as he spoke.

"Yes, Dylan, got it," Seb replied. His feet and his thinking would be his weapons of choice today, and a lot rested on both of them.

CHAPTER 21

The men outside the compound were angry, no—more than that—they were furious. What they thought would be an easy winter in a decent compound was turning into a bloody nightmare.

If only they hadn't killed and tortured those scouts and continued in the direction they were heading in, none of this would have happened.

They knew that someone had gotten into the compound during the night; there were enough bloody corpses around that pointed to that.

Hindsight was a bitch.

The sooner they got inside and gutted whoever was in there, the better off they would be. They could sit in there all winter. They knew there were some women in there, too. They wouldn't kill them; a man needed some company on cold nights after all.

CHAPTER 22

The crack of the shot was much louder than it normally would have been because of how unexpected it was.

"Everyone check in! Who fired?" Dylan yelled into the handheld radio that he had. He had given out as many of them as he could to the people guarding the perimeter of the compound. They weren't much, the batteries were old as dust, but it was the best they could manage.

"Dylan, it's Sam, it was Ben. We just took out the sniper, no time to warn you, over." Sam spoke quickly and calmly into the mike. It was helluva of a shot, and Ben had been waiting for over an hour to take it. Realistically it shouldn't have been that easy to find the sniper, but no doubt he had become careless after no one had put any opposition up over the last few days.

"Okay, nice work," Dylan replied over the radio, "let me know if you see anything else. They will have to make their move sooner or later."

"Roger," said Sam.

"Everyone else, maintain positions, and the second you notice anything unusual, call it in; I don't care how stupid it may seem." A chorus of "yes, okay, and no problem" returned over the radio from the men and women scattered around the compound's walls.

They didn't have to wait long.

The whoosh of a rocket-propelled grenade crashed through the silence; it almost blew the main gates straight off of their hinges. It had seemed like only another second before another one hit the main gates again, knocking one gate down completely, finishing the task.

"Dylan, we have some people approaching the main gate, over." Sam's voice was coming in a calm, professionalism manner shining through.

"Roger, Sam, can you see who the hell fired that RPG?" Dylan yelled into the radio, the long static bursts of automatic rifle fire filling the air.

"Negative on the RPG, but…" Sam's voice was cut off as the sounds of bullets impacting around her ended the transmission.

Dylan looked up toward the tower where Ben and Sam had been positioned; it had been pulverized with rounds, but he could still see movement. Sam threw her pack and Ben's down the ladder, and then waved at Dylan.

"Seb, get someone and get over to the tower, Ben or Sam needs help, now!" Dylan shouted at Seb.

"Okay, okay!" Seb shouted as he ran off in the direction of the tower.

"Matt, come in, Matt, are you there?" Dylan shouted, grabbing his rifle and heading towards the direction of the main gate.

"Um yeah, but I'm kind of busy, buddy. We need help at the main gate. They have knocked the gates down, but so far haven't breached. I have several people injured; not life-threatening, but they need attention," Matt replied, in between letting off several shots.

"Okay, I'm headed there now; Ben and Sam are down, so we have lost our eyes in the sky, Seb is going to check on them," Dylan replied, running in the direction of the main gate.

"Roger!" Matt replied, his voice tense, screaming to be heard over the sounds of automatic fire.

As Dylan ran for the main gate, Matt was firing his pistol in the direction of the main gate, dragging a man by the neck of his shirt out of the line of fire. Another man and woman were covering each other as they fired and then took turns climbing down from the wall.

Just as Dylan had reached Matt, another RPG round whooshed in from the tree line blasting apart a large section of the wall, knocking two of the defenders to the ground. One of them was moving, but the other was motionless.

"Dylan, we got to get off the goddamn walls. We can't stop those rockets, and they're tearing us up!" Matt shouted.

"I know. Okay, everyone, off the walls, now! Fall back to the center of the compound!" Dylan shouted over the radio. There were fewer replies this time than last time.

"Are you okay?" Dylan asked Matt.

"Peachy. You ever had someone shoot a missile at you? I hadn't, until now that is," Matt answered, his sense of humor still intact.

"We can't hold the walls; we need to fall back to the buildings…" Dylan's sentence was interrupted as he brought up his rifle and shot a man who had just run through the gate of the compound.

"I know, let's go!" Matt shouted, throwing the wounded man up over his shoulder and darting off between two of the buildings.

Dylan covered Matt with the rifle but was forced to duck down as a barrage of bullets pounded the wall he was crouched behind. He pointed the rifle around the corner of the building and fired several more shots until the clip clicked on empty. Matt threw the wounded man down behind a low wall, where another member of the compound started to treat his wounds.

"Go, Dylan!" Matt shouted, letting off several well-aimed shots, another attacker fell and was dragged to cover by one of his men.

Dylan didn't stop to look around, sprinting as fast as he could for cover and diving in next to Matt, scraping his face and shoulder in the process.

"Hi!" Matt shouted, letting several more rounds go before his magazine ran dry.

"You have another clip?" Matt asked Dylan.

"Yeah, but this is my last one!" Dylan replied as he reloaded his own rifle. He wasn't even sure how he had managed to go through all five clips of ammunition.

"We have to hold off as long as possible, Ricer shouldn't have been more than a day behind us, and with a little luck his advance element's even closer," Dylan shouted over the sounds of the gunfight raging all around them now.

Just as Dylan went to look around, a man ran around the corner of the building, an AK47 in his hands. He started to bring it up to his shoulder; he was a fraction quicker than Dylan. As bullets started to spew out of the muzzle, kicking up dirt all around Dylan and Matt, an arrow punched through the man's neck, protruding out the other side.

"Dylan! Matt! Are you okay?" Seb asked, his bow in one hand, an arrow in the other.

"Yes, thanks to you! Nice shooting, kid!" Matt replied, but Seb was only staring at the body of the man he had just killed.

"Seb, it's okay, you saved our life. Thank you," Dylan replied, standing up and embracing his younger brother.

"We need to move. Now!" Matt shouted, grabbing his pack and sprinting towards the next building. They were all being pushed into the center of the compound. If help didn't arrive soon Dylan wasn't sure how much longer they would be able to hold out. The group attacking them was much better armed than them and had the experience to go with it.

Matt, Seb, and Dylan threw themselves down behind a barricade that had been constructed outside the main building, the last fallback position. The three were sweating, the sweat cutting streaks through the dirt and grime plastered over their faces.

"Dylan, we need to hold here," one of the scouts was speaking and firing, taking carefully aimed shots, not wasting his ammunition in long, uncontrolled bursts like the attackers.

"I know. How's Ben and Sam?" Dylan asked.

"Sam's okay, just a few scratches, but Ben's gone. He bled out by the time we could get him down from the tower," the scout said quietly. Dylan shook his head and crouched down; it was his fault; he had sent them up there.

"Hey! I know what you're thinking, Dylan, and you can stick it. We all knew the risks; Ben was a soldier, don't take the honor of his sacrifice away from him," the scout replied, gripping Dylan's shoulder tightly as he spoke.

"He's right. Ben knew what he was doing," Sam replied, coming out of the main building, Ben's rifle in her hand.

"I know; I'm glad you're okay," Dylan spoke softly, looking into Sam's blood-smeared face.

"Thanks, but we are in some serious crap now. Ammo is low; we have lost Ben, and three of your people already. If they start shooting any of those rockets in here, I think we need to start considering our options." Sam was looking through the scope of her rifle as she spoke. She pulled the trigger and worked another round into the chamber.

"That's one less, but there are just too many of them, Dylan," she spoke softly, her words quiet but cutting through the sounds of battle around them.

"Sam's right, Dylan. We need to start getting the women and children out of here. They could make it down through the bottom gate," Matt replied, switching clips on his rifle as he spoke. A spray of bullets tore the ground up around them, forcing them all to duck down. Any lower and they would be digging, Dylan thought.

He was about to answer when another rocket whooshed in from somewhere, it glanced off the corner of the building, showering them with stone chips before it shot off into the sky.

"Get the kids and women organized, Seb; Brea will need to lead them out through the bottom gate. I want you to go with them," Dylan said.

"But, I want to stay! I can help. I'm not leaving you and Matt!" Seb shouted.

"I told you that you would do what you're told! You need to take care of Brea, Seb." Dylan knew that it would be hard, but he wanted Seb and his sister out of here, they were all he had left in the world apart from Matt.

"Brea's pregnant!" Seb blurted out, looking at Matt as the words came tumbling out of his mouth.

"What!?" Matt asked, "what did you just say?" He repeated the question.

"She's pregnant. She only found out a little while ago; she made me promise not to tell you," Seb answered him.

"Congratulations, Daddy!" Sam patted him on the back. Dylan hadn't spoken; he was speechless. Among all of this, his sister was going to have a baby; he would be an uncle. Another rocket came tearing into them, this one hitting the wall of the main compound, and blowing a large chunk of the roof and wall away.

"Seb, get in there; make sure everyone is ready to move, now!" Matt screamed at Seb. He was going to be a dad if they made it out of here alive. Seb didn't bother to argue anymore, just started sprinting for the doorway of the building.

The intensity of the automatic fire started to increase, if that was even possible, forcing them to give up the outside position and crowd in on the door of the building.

"Matt, go and check on Brea, make sure she is getting everyone organized. I'll stay here with Sam and cover the door. Brad, get over to the other doorway, grab some of the guys and cover that side of the building—we need to give Seb a chance to lead everyone out of here," Dylan said.

"No problems," Brad replied, double-timing it through the building, tapping a couple of guys on the shoulder as he ran.

CHAPTER 23

The sounds of gunfire and explosions were getting louder, the bark of automatic rifles punching through the forest, with only sporadic reports from larger caliber rifles cutting through every now and again.

"The mother of all battles is going on out there, people, and we need to help!" Ricer shouted to the men and women gathered around him. They had been pushing hard all morning, ever since they had heard the gunfire break through the silence of daybreak.

"Our people, our comrades, our friends are bleeding and dying, and we aren't going to let them die alone! Not today, not while we still have a choice. I don't have time to work out a plan, except get there and get some!" Ricer pumped his fist into the air. A loud cheer answered him, while the soldiers threw down their packs, stripping to just the bare minimum of equipment.

"Now, we are going in hard. Hit them from behind before they realize we are here. This isn't the time for prisoners, just kill them and let's get our people home!" Ricer started running, his people running to catch up with him.

CHAPTER 24

"You ready to go, Seb?" Dylan asked his younger brother.

The people inside the compound's main room were all black and dirty, the smoke and explosions had torn parts of the wall down, and several small fires had been put out.

"Yeah, Dylan, but what about you? We can't leave you!" Seb said.

"You have to. Matt and the rest of us will hold on here, but you need to get Brea and the rest of the women and children out. Just go through the gate and follow the directions on the map that I gave you, we'll catch up as soon as we can," Dylan replied, looking around the room as he spoke.

Matt was huddled down next to Brea, holding her face in his hands, whispering to her and kissing her forehead as he spoke. She was crying, but Dylan knew that as long as she made it out, everything would be worth it. Someone had to live.

The gunfire was intensifying all around them; large chunks of the walls blowing in and spraying the terrified people huddled inside the compound.

"Dylan! They got to go, man! Now!" Matt shouted.

Just as Dylan was about to push Seb to get the hell out, another explosion rocked the building, a large section of the wall giving way over the exit the others were guarding.

"Seb! Get out! Get the hell out of here, now!" Dylan shouted, as a bearded man in camouflage sprayed bullets in through the collapsed section of the building. Matt snapped off a quick shot with his rifle before it clicked on an empty chamber.

Matt cursed under his breath and threw his rifle aside, drawing the pistol from his holster. Seb had the women and children crouched low at the rear of the building, the side facing away from the assault. He had started kicking panels away to reveal a small tunnel which led under the wall and to safety.

Just as Seb started to guide the smaller children and women down through the escape tunnel, the sound of fire increased from outside, but it was somehow different.

Matt looked at Dylan, his eyebrow's raised.

"It's Ricer!" Sam shouted.

"What?" Dylan asked.

"It has to be Ricer and the rest of the patrol. They must be hitting these guys from behind; that's why they're not firing at us as much anymore," Sam said as she kneeled up and fired off another shot at the back of one of the attackers.

"Seb! Wait!" Dylan shouted, but it was still too loud, Seb had just ducked into the tunnel as several members of the compound dragged a large filing cabinet in front of the entrance to the tunnel.

"Matt, you're going to have to head out to the tunnel exit and make sure that it's clear and Seb doesn't get caught up in anything. We'll take care of the stuff here, go!" Dylan shoved Matt as he stood and let several shots go, emptying his pistol clip.

Dylan put the empty pistol back in its holster, with no ammunition it was useless for now, and drew his bow. The fire was coming into the compound still, but the majority was definitely being fired back towards the front of the compound. Dylan was only hoping that Ricer and his people could end this before they were overrun.

"They'll run over them any minute, Dylan. Don't worry; I know my people," Sam said placing her hand on Dylan's shoulder reassuringly. He hadn't realized that his thoughts were that transparent.

"Enough hiding! I'm going out there to help!" Dylan shouted, pulling several arrows out, ready to go.

"Not alone, you're not! Let's help Ricer and get this over and done with. I'll try and cover you from here, just keep low and keep moving!" Sam said, crouching and looking through the scope of the rifle for targets.

"Thanks," Dylan said as he headed for the door. There were only a few people left firing from inside the compound, the rest were either out of ammunition or injured. As he stuck his head out of the doorway for a quick look, the doorway was sprayed with bullets, but not before he saw the man firing blown backward off of his feet, a large hole in his face. Dylan turned to look at Sam, who just gave him a thumbs up and waved, looking back through the scope for more targets.

Dylan looked this time; he just exploded into a fast dash, headed towards the cover of an empty storage shed opposite the doorway. As rounds kicked up dirt around his feet, he dived the last six feet to safety. Dylan crawled into the shelter of the shed's wall, crouched and drawing an arrow, let it fly towards the large attacker reloading across from him. The arrow entered the side of his chest, blowing through the heart, the arrowhead protruding six inches from the other side of his chest.

As he drew another arrow, a bearded man ran around the corner, firing his assault rifle from the hip, rounds spraying in all directions. Dylan brought his bow up and let the arrow fly, the broad-headed arrow slicing clean through one leg and into the other tripping the man, mid-run. Dylan dived on top of him, kicking his pistol away, but not quick enough to prevent the knife to the side.

One of the women from inside the compound ran out and hit the bearded attacker with an ax, almost cutting his head from his neck, blood spraying across Dylan as he clutched his side.

"Goddamn, Connie, thanks. You almost took his bloody head off!" Dylan shouted, the wound in his side starting to really sting.

Connie didn't say anything—just knelt down and vomited on the ground near Dylan.

"It was nothing," she mumbled, wiping the attacker's blood and her own vomit off her face.

"Get back into the compound, I'm okay, but look after the others," Dylan replied picking up his bow and dragging himself up. The fire coming into the compound had ceased, and there seemed to be only sporadic fire coming from the direction of the main gate. Dylan could only hope it was almost over.

A flash out of the corner of his eye had Dylan spinning and dropping into a crouch, his bow automatically coming up.

"Whoa, whoa there, cowboy!" Ricer yelled at Dylan. Dylan lowered the bow and sank back down onto the ground.

"Huh? I knew it was you, Ricer," Dylan replied, dropping the bow onto the ground and lying down next to it.

"Dylan? Dylan? Are you okay?" Ricer asked rushing over to where Dylan had laid down on the ground.

"I am now; I am now. What took you so long?" Dylan asked slowly shutting his eyes and fading off.

"Dylan! Don't go to sleep, buddy. Dylan? Medic!" Ricer shouted.

CHAPTER 25

"Hey there, sleeping beauty!" Matt said as Dylan slowly opened his eyes and looked around. He was in his room; he wasn't dead. He tried to sit up but his body didn't want to do what his brain was telling it to do.

"Whoa, Dylan. The medic said that you shouldn't try to sit up," Brea said, rubbing his arm as she spoke. "The knife went in between your ribs, and there was a lot of bleeding. Also, we dug two bullets out of your leg."

"What happened? Where's Seb?" Dylan started to panic looking around the room and not seeing his younger brother.

"He's fine, Dylan, Matt found him outside the camp with the children, and got a bat to the back of the head for his trouble!" Ricer replied, not even bothering to try and stifle the loud laugh.

"Shut up," Matt said, rubbing his head and frowning.

"Yeah, one of the kids was the look out and caught Matt trying to 'sneak up' on them, so he hit him with a baseball bat!" Brea said, even she was giggling now.

"What happened with the attack? Did you get them all?" Dylan asked.

"We lost a few people, and some of yours were just too injured. All the attackers are dead; we hung the last one this morning," Ricer replied looking down, there had been too much death and destruction, his country needed to heal, not turn on itself.

"Thank you, I mean it, thank you, Ricer," Dylan spoke softly trying to reach out for Ricer, a tear rolling down his cheek.

"No problem. But we do have a problem," Ricer said.

"What, what's the matter?" Dylan asked, concern creeping into his voice.

"Well, between your injuries, your people's and mine, we aren't going anywhere. It snowed this morning while you were sleeping. Not just a dusting either; there must be at least two or three feet of snow out there. We are all going to get mighty neighborly around here in the next month or so!" Ricer replied, a smile creeping across his face. Everyone in the room started laughing and hugging. No matter how bad things were it couldn't get any worse than what they had gone through the last couple of months.

"Wouldn't have it any other way!" Dylan replied, shaking Ricer's hand.

The End.

If you enjoyed the book I would appreciate your review on Amazon!

Please make sure to follow me on Goodreads or Facebook.

www.facebook.com/BenandSamAuthors/